Oh Honey

by
Emily R. Austin

Holland House

www.hhousebooks.com

Paperback ISBN: 978-1-910688-25-0
Kindle: 978-1-910688-26-7

Cover design by Julia B. Lloyd

Typeset by Julia B. Lloyd

Published in the USA, Canada and UK

Holland House Books
Holland House
47 Greenham Road
Newbury, Berkshire RG14 7HY
United Kingdom

www.hhousebooks.com

For Ms Nedic

Oh Honey

"Hello, my name is Esther. I am calling on behalf of Krippler Incorporated, a market research institute. Today we are conducting a survey on feline diabetes. Do you, or any member of your household, own a cat?"

They hang up.

"Hello. My name is Joan. I am calling on behalf of—"

They hang up.

"Hello. My name's Doreen."

***

I am having a hard time enjoying my break because my tea is green. I am concerned because the packet said that it was orange pekoe. I am not sure if tea names should correspond with their colour. For example, is Earl Grey really grey? I have no idea.

Maybe there was an innocent mislabelling incident at the tea factory, and my orange pekoe is merely disguised green tea. Or perhaps this particular brand of orange pekoe contains an unusual ingredient that discolours the product. Really, there exists an abundance of plausible explanations.

The possibility remains, however, that I could be drinking brewed mold. Should a person willingly consume a substance that could potentially be brewed mold? A thought-provoking question, worthy of a research paper. Sadly I am short for time, and potently uninterested in the subject.

Swishing what could be fermented fungus around in my gullet, I wonder whether ingesting mildew might produce a high. This pondering prompts me to drink my "orange pekoe" with a little more zeal.

After a hearty swig, I conclude that I do not feel any sort of mold-induced euphoria. What I feel could be aptly classified as nausea. It remains unclear whether my nausea is a consequence of my beverage choice or whether it is just another one of my body's ways of expressing self-hatred.

I am trying not to smoke because I am unhealthy. I sit in a cubical for eight hours every day and my diet is primarily determined by the man who stocks the staffroom vending machines. I recently winded myself trying to shovel a spoonful of ice cream from an exceptionally frozen carton. As I gasped for air, I resolved to make a lifestyle change. I can accept being unable to run a marathon. I can accept the prospect of a premature death. I can even accept becoming one of those morbidly obese people who monopolizes the motorized shopping carts, slighting the elderly and the justly physically handicapped. I cannot, however, consent to an existence in which I am incapable of serving myself Cherry Garcia.

Tea, I've read, is healthy. Smoking, disappointingly, is not. Thus, I am attempting to exchange habits.

I regret my experimentation with tea. Besides being inexplicably green, the tea bag ripped when I stirred it too enthusiastically, and now bits of the ground leaves are floating in the boiling water, reminiscent of drowned bugs. When I swallow they lodge themselves in my oesophagus.

I have decided that this dark tea period in my life is going to be cut short. The lack of cigarettes in my system is making a sizeable portion of my insides fester.

Maybe I am an exception, and cigarettes are actually good for me. Bodies scab to heal wounds, they repair broken bones. The human body wants nothing more than to be healthy. Why, then, would mine express such a consuming need for a cigarette?

The only sensible answer is that cigarettes are wholesome and nourishing.

I stare at my green, seemingly bug-filled mug, and listen to my stomach sing a song about indigestion. In an attempt to silence the unwelcome gurgle-hymn that erupts from the crypt of my being, I contort myself inelegantly.

One of my co-workers is also sitting in the staff room. He sees my strange movements and shoots me an impolite look.

"Can I help you?" I confront him loudly.

Startled by my assertiveness, he recoils. He pretends that he didn't hear me, and suddenly appears to be bizarrely fascinated by the office microwave. He stares fixedly at the buttons and runs his thumb along its door.

Unimpressed by every experience the past ten minutes has offered me, I decide to abandon my mug of what claims to be tea. I leave the break room and walk outside to execute a lineup of three cigarettes in succession.

***

After three taxing hours of being unremittingly hung up on, I decide that it is time for a pick-me-up. Whenever I feel especially downtrodden at work I call the man who hates me. Telemarketing is by its nature a soul-crushing vocation, so I am habitually downtrodden. I call the man who hates me at least once per shift. I once called him twenty-two times.

I have his number inscribed on a pink, daisy-shaped post-it note. I have secured the note to the top of my computer screen for quick reference. All of the zeros are heart-shaped, and the note is festooned with small decorative stars.

"Why have you got his number wrote like that?" Frank, my developmentally challenged friend who sits in the cubical next to mine, asks me. "Do you like him?"

"Of course I don't like him, Frank," I begin to clarify. "It's satirical. The innocent girlish note is designed to deliberately contrast with this man's fully-grown virile anger, offering a subtle criticism on his treatment of sales employees, and potentially also women—" I pause.

It's ringing.

"Hello?"

"Hello. My name is Marla. I am calling on behalf of—"

His throat produces a gurgling noise when he is upset.

"STOP IT!" he screams. "How many goddamn times do I have to tell you people to stop calling me!"

He shouts right off the bat. He does not grow gradually to anger, like most people do. He is immediately irate.

"Please let me assure you that I am not selling anything."

"I don't care if you're giving away free plutonium, you unimaginable whore! I have asked that these calls cease!"

He hangs up.

***

The elevator in my apartment whines while it lifts me. It cries in its elevator tongue that it is in desperate need of repairs.

"I am in desperate need of repairs," it bawls.

Though fluent in the language of the lift, I am no elevator doctor. I cannot cure this sorry machinery of the disorder that plagues it. I do, however, possess the imagination of a gifted child, and I can therefore diagnose it.

Elevator Huntington's disease, a rare and malignant elevator condition with symptoms that occasionally include plummeting rapidly to the bottom of the elevator shaft, horrifically mangling all passengers.

The prospect of dying inside of this moving metal coffin does not sit well with me. Imminent death in general actually sits quite well with me, but this is not how I wanted to go. I don't want to die because I was too lazy to take the stairs.

The elevator's protestations have grown increasingly shrill.

I imagine the cables breaking and myself and the elevator free-falling.

I then imagine it breaking and stopping, and having to sleep on the carpet until some gallant firemen come to salvage me from the wreckage. I then look at the ground below my feet. At the stains on the floor.

I wonder if anyone has ever had sex in this elevator.

I wonder if anyone has ever done drugs in this elevator.

I then remember that I have had sex and done drugs in this elevator.

***

To my surprise, I reach the tenth floor alive. I exit the elevator with a rejuvenated gratitude for my continued life.

My cause of death will not be poorly maintained apartment facilities. I plan to expire at the culmination of an odyssey of drugs, like any decent human being. My obituary will be worth cutting out of the newspaper and magnetizing to the fridge. The men who conduct my autopsy will have something worth discussing at the dinner table that night ("Kids, today we worked on a body that contained more LSD than was previously thought to have existed on the planet.") Hundreds of pages of poetry will be composed about the romantic offing of me. The story of my death will win a Pulitzer Prize. Youths will study it in college. Thousands of years from now it will be scripture: The Holy Book of Jane's Overdose.

I trudge towards my apartment, ready to tell my roommate Keats to stay clear of the broken elevator.

"Hey Keats," I shout upon entry, "stay clear of the broken elevator."

Keats is sitting at the kitchen table, wearing oversized headphones, poring over old newspapers and wielding a green highlighter. He is too engrossed in his task to look up at me.

He is chewing on the end of the highlighter and mumbling quietly to himself.

I watch him for a few seconds before he looks up and notices me. When he does notice me, he jolts up out of his chair and begins frantically gathering the newspapers off the table. He thrusts the highlighter away from himself like it's a javelin.

"What are you up to?" I ask him.

"Nothing," he replies, which is undoubtedly suspicious.

My level of interest remains low nonetheless, so I reply:

"That's cool."

***

I cut an avocado in half and roll the pit round in the palm of my hand. The green residue coats my hands and gets in between my fingers. The pit slips from my grip and falls into the recycling box below, crashing clamorously against the empty soup and soda cans.

I hear Keats whimper from the couch.

"Jane?" he yelps, his voice hoarse.

He had fallen asleep.

"Jane?" he says again, louder this time.

"Sorry," I murmur.

"Thank God. I thought you were the police," he breathes, relieved.

"Why would I be the police?" I wipe my hands off on my shirt.

"Because," he scoffs, "I'm involved in some things."

I bring my avocado innards into the living room and drop down into the seat next to his.

Keats is a conspiracy theorist. He is convinced that his every misfortune is the direct outcome of a nationwide attempt to ruin him. The government, big corporations, his family—all want nothing more than to undermine and control him.

"How was your day?" I query politely.

"Well, I didn't get that job at Taco Bell," he answers, dejected. "But you know what? I am almost sure it's because Taco Bell is run by the same people who are responsible for the Armenian genocide."

I press my lips together for a moment. "Are you suggesting that Mexico had anything to do with—?"

He cackles. "Mexicans? Don't kid yourself, Jane. Taco Bell is run by the Germans."

"You think that the Germans are responsible for the Armenian genocide?"

He taps his nose.

I then say quietly, mostly to myself, "You think that Germans are responsible for Crunchwrap Supremes?"

***

"Hello, my name is Belle. I am calling on behalf of—"

They hang up.

"Hello, my name is Ariel. I am calling behalf of Krippler Incorporated, a market research institute. Today we are conducting—"

"On behalf of wha'?" replies a woman with a heavy southern accent.

"On behalf of Krippler Incorporated, a market research institute."

"Wha's tha'?"

"It is, uh, a market research institute."

"Where are you calling from?"

"We are located in Ottawa," I recite.

"Where?"

"Ottawa, the capital city of Canada."

"Oh," she says, sleepy, "never heard of it."

Then she hangs up.

"Hello. My name is Pocahontas. I am calling on behalf of—"

"Pocawhat?" repeats the respondent.

"Pocahontas. I am calling on behalf of Krippler Incorporated—"

"That ain't no name."

"No it is," I assure him. "Today we are conducting a

7

survey—"

"Yer parents hippies or wha'?"

"Aboriginal," I answer. "Our survey today is on feline diabetes."

"I ain't talking to no hip—" he begins to say as he hangs up.

Disheartened by everyone hanging up on me, I decide that it is time to cheer myself up. I touch the post-it note adhered to my computer screen and dial the number. I listen to it ringing while absentmindedly twirling the phone cord in my fingers, in the same way that prepubescent girls do when they call a boy that they have a crush on.

"Hi Billy, this is Sarah calling from your English class. Janey said you like me, is that true?"

"Excuse me?"

"I'm calling on behalf of Krippler—"

He hangs up.

"Hello?"

"Hello this is Aurora calling on behalf of Krippler Incorp—"

"NO!" the man promptly begins shrieking. "You Godforsaken cretins have called me every Goddamn day for the past fortnight!"

"Please accept my apology—"

"I absolutely will not accept anything from you! You can remove me from your calling list!"

I look down at my calling list and recite: "We do not have a calling list, sir."

"Liar!" he explodes. "You are absolutely lying! I demand your name!"

I forget which name I gave him.

"Your name!" he repeats.

"Jane."

"Why don't you go out and get yourself a real job, Jane? Why don't you go to school? Why don't you become a contributing member of society!"

"Please let me assure you that I am not selling anything—"

"I hope you rot in hell!" he screeches as he hangs up.

***

I would not be astounded to discover that Krippler Incorporated is actually Hell. I find it difficult to envision a place more hellish than a labyrinth of grey cubicles populated by depressed, robotic-speaking smokers collectively responding graciously to a never-ending lineup of people telling them to fuck off. I suspect that Hell is also decorated with dusty synthetic ferns and yellowed motivational posters. I would certainly not be surprised to discover that Satan himself is responsible for the incessant buzzing noise that rains persistently down from the fluorescent lights above me.

***

I am spending my lunch break in the hoary back alley of Krippler Incorporated, in exile with my fellow smokers. Communally exhaling, we have created an imposing white cloud of tobacco and condensation over our heads. It looms there, joining the looming repentance and remorse we probably all share.

Snow has coated my hair like icing and my fingertips feel anaesthetized. The frigid outside has prompted me to toy once again with the idea of quitting smoking, but then how will I slowly kill myself?

I am accompanied by two women who both possess unmemorable names. One of the two women has the face of a person who has done heroin. The other of the two women has the face of a regular person, who has likely never done heroin. Frank is also standing with us, but he does not smoke.

Heroin-face asks us, "Are you guys getting many interviews?"

Regular-face answers, "Yeah, a couple."

I reply, "A few."

Frank nods. "I got a couple too." Then he chuckles. "This one guy—"

Heroin-face interrupts him before he can finish his sentence. She says, "This is the worst job I've ever had." She then inhales half her cigarette in one go.

Frank does not attempt to finish his story. He looks down at his feet, defeated.

I glare at the woman as she exhales, bothered by her mistreatment of Frank.

Regular-face nods. "You're telling me. It's a soulless job."

I nod too. "Totally."

"I used to dance," heroin-face shares. This doesn't really surprise me. "I got too old for that though."

I smile weakly at her sad, drug-assaulted face. "What are you talking about? You don't look a day over nineteen."

She grins at me. "Thank you, baby."

Nineteen million.

"I used to work for a pet store," Frank tells us, looking up from his feet. He shakes his head. "I got fired for stealing pens."

***

I have buttoned my blouse all the way up my neck in preparation for my probation meeting. I did this in an effort to present myself as meek and upright; however, all I have succeeded in doing is presenting myself as breathless. My humble and unassertive outfit is gently depriving me of oxygen. Seemingly distraught by being draped over my immodest body, the unyielding grip of my collar is softly strangling me.

"So how are things?" Asks my probation counselor, who is dressed in a low-cut breathable smock.

"Good." I smile, covertly resentful of her comfortable collarline.

"How's work?"

"Good," I say again, still smiling. Still being strangled.

She begins to read a list of my prescribed medications.

"So, you're on Lithium, Fluvoxamine, and Clozapine?"

"Yes," I nod, internally resisting a powerful compulsion to tear the buttons off my shirt.

"And are you taking anything else?" She locks her pupils with mine.

"Absolutely—" I gasp for air "—not."

***

"Jane!"

After returning home from my probation meeting, I laid down on the floor of my bedroom. Weak and frail from breathing inadequately for hours, I concluded that walking the extra meter to my bed would be too strenuous an exercise.

Cushioned by the piles of clothing that I have amassed on my carpet and sedated by a fistful of Clozapine, I accidently dozed off.

"Jane!"

"What?" I stir, winded.

Keats' girlfriend, Ivy, pushes my door open. It fights against my mounds of laundry.

"As per usual, Jonathan's asleep", she complains while positioning one of my hoodies under her head and lying down beside me.

She always refers to Keats by his first name.

"Typical Jonathan." I rub my eyes.

"I hope that you don't mind me hanging out here anyways," she says, without pausing for me to interject with my feelings on the subject. "I just cannot stay at my parent's house for even a moment longer."

"Not even a moment, eh?"

"Let me ask you something," she continues, "what do your parents do?"

"My parents are dead."

"Oh Jane. I'm so sorry," she stammers.

"That's okay. They died a long time ago."

"How long ago?"

"I was thirteen. They both died of a pretty rare disease. It was eventually named after them, actually. Jerry and Sheryl Syndrome. Maybe you've heard of it?"

She shakes her head.

"It's pretty rare."

She begins to extend her arm out towards me, apparently aiming to touch my hand in some sort of gesture of awkward sympathy.

I dodge her touch and say, "They were pharmacists before they died though, to answer your question. Really great pharmacists, too. Critically acclaimed. Why did you ask?"

"Oh," she breathes, "because my dad owns a car wash." She rolls her eyes. "A fucking car wash. And you'd think it washed AIDS cure, the way he talks about it. Every conversation I have ever had with my father has revolved around the Ottawa City Car Wash. Can you even imagine?"

"I can't."

"My sisters and I spend every family dinner sitting silently listening to my parents delude themselves about that stupid car wash. They think it's the most interesting place on earth, I swear. And my mom just hangs on my dad's every word about it. She encourages him! She says stuff like, 'Really, honey? Wow a Porsche came in today?'" she mimics her mother's voice, which is apparently comically high-pitched. "I just want to scream shut up, you know? I just want to fucking scream that no one gives a shit about the car wash."

"Then do it." I advise.

She laughs. "Yeah, right. Would you say that to your dad?"

I shrug. "Yes."

***

Keats has awoken from his ritual mid-day nap and has come to accompany me and Ivy in my room. The three of us are now lying on my bedroom floor, taking turns with a sixty of tepid beer, a cigarette, and a joint. I am now in possession of the beer.

Keats is discussing tomatoes.

"Anyone who would willingly eat a genetically modified tomato deserves a medal for stupidity. A medal."

Ivy nods. "Totally."

I consider the sum of money I would be willing to bet that Ivy has no idea what genetically modified food is.

"But what are we supposed to do?" Keats continues, impassioned. "We can buy organic, sure. Sure, if the food labeled organic were actually organic. It's just a sticker used to up the price tag." He exhales loudly. "We are all under the oppressive rule of Monsanto. Modern day peasants living under the tyranny of the corporate kings. We might as well brand ourselves with barcodes."

"Yeah, like what even is organic?" Ivy adds insightfully as she tugs the sixty from my grip, apparently fervent for her turn with it.

This causes her to inadvertently move the sleeve of my sweater up my arm.

"Speaking of branding," she murmurs while I pull away from her.

Keats' eyes dart to my arm.

I like to press sharp objects against myself and bleed. I consider this a recreational activity that has little to no negative ramifications on my everyday life. The one setback I have experienced is that people who see the marks either interpret them as a cry for help or for attention. I then receive their unwanted pity, or their judgement for being attention-seeking. The subject is embarrassing. I just like the sensation, and I believe that I should be able to amputate my own hand if I am so compelled. I am the sole owner of all of my own appendages.

I scowl at Ivy while I pull my sleeve back down.

"Some of those look pretty fresh, Jane," Keats says in his angry voice.

Keats expresses his affection for me by acting in an inappropriately paternal way. Though I can appreciate that the sentiment is coming from a loving place, Keats is derisorily underqualified to be my father.

I take a drag from the cigarette.

"Jane…" Ivy says in a vexed tone that irks me and makes me want to punch her in the face.

"Hush," I say to them both calmly, trying to remain in control of my cool.

I am the master of my cool.

"You know that we both care about you, right?" Ivy says softly.

I cringe. "Every expression of emotion is overly sentimental and a reflection of one's stupidity, Ivy."

"Why do you do that to yourself?" Keats asks me loudly. "Why?"

I imagine force-feeding Keats genetically modified tomatoes.

"Why?" he demands again.

"I do it entirely to trouble you," I sneer, losing my grip on my cool.

"Well consider me troubled!" He flings the roach of the joint onto my bedroom floor and storms out of the room.

"I already consider you troubled," I say before he marches fully out of sight.

***

In direct response to the unsolicited meddling of Keats and Ivy, I have tinted my bath water rosy with the happy colouring of my insides. I move my legs rapidly under the water to create waves. I am Moses reincarnated, turning this tub into the Red Sea. Bringing God's almighty wrath onto this unholy washroom. The rubber ducky cowers in my presence. My wrists bleed like I'm Christ.

***

Frank came into work today proudly clutching a new pen to gift me with. He placed it delicately in front of me on my desk, like a religious offering. The words "Larry's Famous Pet Store" are emblazoned on its side, and its cap is shaped like the head of a dog.

"Is this for me?"

He nods. "Yup."

"You shouldn't have."

***

A woman is taking my survey.

"Feline diabetes, gosh!"

She exhales loudly down the phone.

"Yeah, pretty heavy stuff." I yawn. "Do you, or any member of your household, own a cat?"

"Yes, I have four cats."

I code "yes" into my computer.

"And what are their ages?"

"Dwayne is eighteen, Desmond is ten, Dixie is also ten, and Muffin is two." She laughs. "And I know what you're thinking, who names their cat Muffin? Well, let me tell you, if you saw her you'd see how well it suits her."

I try to imagine a cat that looks like a muffin.

"Do any of them have pre-existing health problems?" I ask.

"Mhm. Dwayne is completely blind. Can you believe that? He's totally blind. Gets around totally on smells. Isn't that just remarkable?"

"Yeah," I say, "that's pretty impressive, sure."

"And Desmond's got liver problems, which is what normally kills cats. Did you know that?"

"I didn't."

Everything I know about cats derives fully from this survey.

"Excuse me for just a minute, miss," she says, "I have to go turn my television down. The news keeps reporting on this awful story about a homicidal boy."

"That's fine," I tell her.

"Have you heard about that?"

"About what?"

"This kid who murdered his whole family," she sighs.

"That's terrible."

"It's grotesque. The news is always reporting on the horror stuff. For once I'd like to hear a pleasant story. You know?"

"Yeah, maybe something on a blind cat," I suggest.

She giggles. "Wouldn't that be neat?"

"Gets around totally on smells," I say under my breath, imagining that I am the reporter.

***

"Hello, my name is Mallory. I am calling on behalf of—"

"You must be joking!"

"Krippler Incorporated. Today we are conducting a survey on feline diabetes—"

"You goddamn impudent excuses for human beings have called my household relentlessly for weeks! I demand your employee number!"

"I don't have an employee number."

"Preposterous! There is no reputable company—" he stops himself. "Oh, of course you don't have an employee number. Of course Krippler Incorporated, enterprise of the depraved, doesn't abide by Goddamn rudimentary business principles!"

"Our survey today is on feline diabetes." I press on. "Do you, or any member of your household, own a cat?"

He hangs up.

***

"Hello, my name is Ainsley. I am calling on behalf of—"

"Ainsley? Or is this Jane again?"

"My apologies, yes, this is Jane calling on behalf of Krippler Incorporated. Today we are conducting—"

"A survey on cat diabetes," the man finishes my sentence.

"Exactly yes." I continue. "Do you or any member of your household own a cat?"

"Are you suicidal, Jane?" he asks me calmly. "Are you?" he repeats, the volume of his voice increasing. "Because I sense that you may be. Why else would you continue to call a man who has expressed in no uncertain terms his disdain for your calls? Are you trying to oblige someone to kill you so you don't have to, Jane? Is that the master plan, Jane? Too goddamn craven to commit the act yourself?"

I stifle a laugh at the implication that I am thoughtful enough to execute that intricate a suicide.

"Do you or any member of your household own a cat?" I repeat.

"Do you own a death wish?" he asks.

"Perhaps a Tabby?" I propose. "Maybe a Burmese?"

He hangs up.

***

Heroin-face sighs vociferously. "I wish I could find a new job."

She, Frank, and I are standing amid a small band of smokers outside.

"I can't find anything new though." She shakes her head.

I am not sure who she is directing these remarks at. None of the women around us are responding to her. Their deadpan faces all stare through her, unmoved.

She lowers her voice and leans in. "It's very hard to find yourself a good job when you've got yourself a criminal record."

Suddenly the group's interest is kindled. The women's glassy, impassive expressions have all metamorphosed. Everyone seems suddenly invigorated by the opportunity to gossip about the misfortunes of this sad, dissolute woman.

Frank's face remains unresponsive. This, I feel, reflects well on his character. He was not interested in her before she disclosed her criminal past, and he remains unconcerned now.

One of the ladies says tightly: "You have a criminal record? Oh gosh. That's bad."

I for one do not find heroin-face's lawless past particularly astounding. Perhaps I am a good judge of character. Perhaps her neck tattoo gave her away.

Heroin-face nods. "Yup. Prison really changes a person, let me tell you."

"That's true." I nod.

"Have you been to prison?" She slurs loudly, turning to me.

The crowd of women rapidly shift to become my audience. All of their impatient eyes are now directed at me. I feel like I am dangling feed in front of a ravenous brood of hens.

After taking a deliberately drawn-out drag from my cigarette, I nod nonchalantly. "Yeah, I have."

I watch as their jaws fall collectively open.

"What were you in for?" one of them asks me, speaking so hastily that her words seem to blend.

This is an impolite question, but seeing as this woman has probably never been imprisoned herself I realize that she is probably unfamiliar with jail-themed etiquette. You can't expect people to keep their elbows off the table if they have only ever eaten off the floor.

"I took a man hostage." I inhale. "He was a nameless criminal, originally from Costa Rica. He was involved in some identity larceny, a little human trafficking, subornation, and so forth. He ended up involving a close friend of mine, and I had to make the decision to do something a little impetuous. It landed me in jail for a respectable percentage of my childhood, but you make sacrifices, right?"

One of the women stares. "That sounds complicated."

I scratch my chin. "It was pretty simple actually, but yeah."

***

"Hello my name is Aaron. I am calling on behalf of Krippler Incorporated. Today—"

"Are you kidding me?"

"Today we are conducting a survey on feline diabetes. Do you or any member of your household own a cat?"

"You have already called my household twice this evening, Jane," the man articulates pointedly. "Twice!" he repeats. "And I have requested each time that you never ever call me again. What exactly is your motive here? Why exactly are you doing this to me?"

"Do you or any member of your household own a cat?"

He begins to laugh maniacally. "You really are something, aren't you, Jane?"

"Our survey today is on feline diabetes," I continue.

"How would you like it if I harassed you in your home every day? Hmm? How would you like that?"

"Do you or any member of your household own a cat?"

"You are vile, scum of the earth."

***

On the nights when Ivy is not sleeping over at our apartment, she has taken to calling me and talking to me for the duration of the evolution of man. I sit aging on the phone while the stars above me begin burning out. Whole species of animals become endangered and extinct at my feet.

I find myself swapping my phone from one ear to the other, to avoid permanently deadening one. Though upon deeper analysis, it might be cunning to deliberately deafen myself in order to make future phone calls with Ivy bearable.

I occasionally put my phone down on my bed and walk away, only to return to Ivy's oblivious continued rambling. I make numerous attempts to hang up, all of which are futile.

"Ivy, I need to go eat something now. I will have to let you go."

"We can keep chatting while you eat. I don't mind hearing people eat."

"Ivy, listen, I need to use the washroom. I will have to let you go."

"K, I'll call you back in five."

"Ivy, listen, I am in the middle of being murdered by an axe-wielding lunatic. I am afraid I will have to let you go."

My theory is that she does it to listen to the background noises of our apartment. She is scanning for female voices. She says that she does it because she wants us to become better friends, but I am not so easily fooled. She thinks Keats—gaunt, unemployed, and devoid of charm Keats—is, miraculously, entertaining a myriad of ladies on the sly.

"Have you ever had an abortion?" she interviews me. Moments before we were discussing our mutual affection for domesticated pigs. The conversation did not transition to abortion seamlessly.

"Why?" I ask, concerned now that Ivy is with child.

The unnerving image of a child with the morphed features of Ivy's blank Barbie-doll face positioned on Keats' gangly body begins to form, unwelcome, in my mind.

"Oh, I just wondered," she explains. "So, you've never had an abortion then?"

"No, actually. I have."

"Really? When?"

"When I was kid," I tell her.

"A kid?" she repeats.

"A teenager," I clarify, "I was about thirteen."

"Thirteen? Really? That's so young, Jane. Were you raped?"

"What? No. It wasn't anything like that."

"Thirteen is so young though." She emphasizes the word "so", as if I were under the false impression that thirteen-year-olds collect pensions. As if I believed that I'd had an abortion late in my life.

"Is it?" I say.

She says nothing.

"Have you ever had one?" I ask her.

"Yeah, I had one when I was in grade twelve."

I say nothing.

"What was your first time like?" she asks me after a moment of silence that I bleakly interpret as being in memoriam of our unborn.

"Um. Pretty normal."

"Who was the boy?"

"His name was Ethan," I lie. His name was Mr. Arwol. I never learned what his first name was. "He was on the basketball team. His parents were both lawyers. He always wore those shiny, purple Nike shorts. Do you remember those? I guess maybe they were cool at the time. Looking back he didn't exactly scream 'I am the person who should take your virginity' but que sera, sera, am I right?"

She breathes air out of her nose. "That's funny."

"What was your first time like?" I ask her.

"It sucked." She snorts. "My boyfriend had no idea what he was doing. He broke the clasps on my bra trying to take it off. It was especially depressing because I had just spent hours at the mall that day picking out just the right bra. I spent like eighty dollars on it. We had been dating for like six months though, so it was sort of expected, you know? How long had you been dating Ethan?"

I stare the creases in my knuckles. "About two months," I lie.

She laughs. "Whoa Jane. You whore."

I laugh. "Yeah. Total whore."

Mr. Arwol and I were not dating at all.

***

Mr. Arwol was my neighbour, and the father of the child that I babysat. He had a receding hairline and a stomach that protruded from the summit of his pants, like a rising muffin. He smelled like laundry detergent and banana medicine.

I initiated it. I put my small, not yet fully grown hand on his middle-aged thigh. My nails were ornamented with glitter polish that matched one of my dolls, and my wrists were elegantly wreathed with seahorse-shaped Silly Bandz.

He was wearing dress pants with ironed-in creases. These had probably been lovingly made by his doting wife. She was a tired-looking blonde woman who overpaid me.

I ran my finger along a crease, flattening it against his skin.

I thought we might just make out. I was unacquainted with sexual logistics.

No condom.

No birth control.

No period that month.

***

"Hello my name is Emma Woodhouse, I am calling on behalf of—"

They hang up.

"Hello my name is Harriet Smith. I am calling on behalf of—"

They hang up.

"Hello my name is Jane Fairfax. I am calling on behalf of—"

***

"I absolutely insist that you stop calling me!" The man who I keep calling roars deafeningly into his receiver. "For the love of God and of all that is holy, I demand that you stop!"

"Do you or any members of your household own a cat?"

"I am in a business meeting, you wretched, reprehensible woman! Do you have any idea what it's like to be persistently interrupted by unsolicited phone calls whilst attempting to conduct one's business?"

"We're conducting a survey on feline diabetes."

"Are you suffering from some sort of cerebral frailty, Jane? Is severe retardation perhaps at the root of our repeated miscommunication? Or does this stem from some sort of feminine irrationality?"

***

Keats bursts into my room in a tsunami of body odour. Startled by his unexpected entrance and irritated that he didn't knock, I open my mouth to yell at him. Before my vocal apparatus has had a chance to engage, however, I manage to stop myself.

Keats responds poorly to anger. It is best that I internalize my feelings. With any luck they will manifest themselves as cancer instead, which will hopefully then kill me. Thus, ultimately, my goal of avoiding living this experience ever again might be accomplished anyway.

I notice that Keats is accompanied by a sizable bottle of vodka as well as an equally sizable joint. Though his presence remains unwelcomed, I theorize that these items will make it possible for me to console myself.

He sits down beside me with his legs crossed and rips the plastic cap off of the vodka bottle using only his teeth. Spitting the cap across my room, he sighs and says, "Are you aware of the relationship between the assassination of President Lincoln and the Vatican?"

I stare at him.

"Remarkably, no, Keats," I answer dully.

"I've been writing down all of the things that Lincoln said that were anti-Catholic," he licks his lips, "and I've also been reading about an ex-priest named Charles Chiniquy. Have you heard of him? Let me tell you, Jane—"

"Hey Keats," I interrupt him, desperate to evade hearing any more on the subject, "what was your first time like?"

I have chosen this question because the subject is fresh in my memory.

He swigs from the bottle and grins. "My first time for what? Sex?"

Perhaps I was too quick to change the subject. Maybe I would prefer to hear conspiracies about the Vatican than learn anything about Keats' sordid sexual past.

"No. I meant the first time someone mistook you for a Proboscis monkey."

"The first time I had sex was pretty good, thank you for asking, Jane. Mayla Brasman had me over to her house. Her parents were away in Europe. She had candles lit." He shakes his head and repeats, "Mayla Brasman."

"She sounds great." I stare lifelessly at the ceiling.

"She was great. Quite great, actually. She had bought this outfit too," he beams at me, "it was all lacy."

I hold my hand up to communicate that I would like him to stop.

"Red lace," he continues, despite my polite indication not to. "Red lace that I tore to pieces by the end of the evening. You know, I think that lingerie manufacturers intentionally use fabrics that can't withstand even moderately aggressive sex. They know it's going to get torn off the woman. They know it needs to be durable, and yet they keep using these flimsy fabrics that essentially disintegrate under the strain of even mild petting."

I reach for the vodka.

"You can barely kiss a girl wearing lingerie without destroying it. You know, they do it so that women have to re-buy and re-buy the damn things. It's a marketing tactic designed to ensure that the lingerie corporations keep getting their precious money. It's appalling, when you think about it."

"The gall of those underwear stores," I say between sips.

"Right? Women should boycott underwear stores, if you ask me."

I nod. "Yeah. Go tell women to stop wearing underwear, Keats. You should take this cause on."

He chuckles. "When was your first time?"

"Middle school," I lie.

"And who was the lucky guy?"

"His name was Cameron," I reply. "He was the head of the chess team."

"The chess team, eh?" Keats smirks.

"That's right, he was smart. He went on to get a PhD in biomedical engineering, actually. I think he even published a couple textbooks for an introductory university course he taught. He started teaching when he was only nineteen. Maybe eighteen, actually. A real child prodigy, that guy."

"Wow," Keats says, impressed.

"Yeah." I nod.

***

"Hello my name is Scout Finch. I am calling on behalf of—"
They hang up.

"Hello my name is Jo March. I am calling on behalf of—"
They hang up.

"Hello my name is Hester Prynne. I am calling on behalf of—"
They hang up.

"Hello my name is Sara Crewe. I am calling on behalf of—"
They hang up.

"Hello my name is Anne Shirley. I am calling on behalf of—"
They hang up.

***

"Hello my name is Christina. I am calling on behalf of Krippler Incorporated. Today—"

"No way! This is Christina? How you been, girl?" The respondent answers delighted, evidently confusing me for a friend of hers whose name is actually Christina.

"Uh. Good," I respond gingerly. "I'm conducting a survey."

"A survey? This for school?"

"N—Yes," I answer. "It is about feline diabetes. Do you or any member of your household own a cat?"

"Are you kidding me, Christina? You know damn well I don't own any cats! You think Franco would let me keep a reeking cat in his house?"

I pretend to laugh knowingly. "Ha. Ha, yes, of course old Franco wouldn't allow such a thing. What was I thinking?"

She snorts. "No kidding, girl! So how are your kids? Is Kendrick in school now?"

"Yes," I reply. "Kendrick's just started school this year, actually."

"Wow, time sure flies, eh?" the woman sighs.

"It sure does."

"Well hey listen Christina, I've got some chicken cooking in my oven. I am gunna have to let you go, alright? It was so good to hear from you though. You'll call me again, will ya?"

"Sure."

"Alright. Love you, girl! Bye!"

"Bye. I love you too."

***

"Have you been using that pen I got for you?" Frank asks me while leaning informally on the cubical wall that separates our desks.

"I have been, yes." I nod.

"And how do you like it?" he asks coolly.

"It's great. It writes smooth."

He laughs haughtily. "Yeah, I thought you would probably like it."

***

"You look very put-together today, Jane," my probation counselor remarks after thoroughly eyeing me up and down.

"Thank you." I smile, fidgeting uncomfortably under the strain of her scrutiny. "You look very put-together today too."

"Thank you." She smiles back at me. "You're also looking very healthy. Have you been taking good care of yourself?"

"I have been, thank you, yes," I lie, smoothing out the lap of my dress. "I have been very into kale lately. Do you ever eat kale?"

I read an article in the lobby about kale.

She shakes her head. "No, I've actually never tried kale."

"I put it in my smoothies," I lie. "Sometimes I dry it out, season it, and make chips. It is very versatile, kale."

"Oh really? Well, it sounds great."

"It is. It has got omega-3 fatty acid."

My only recent sustenance has come out of a family-sized box of Pop Tarts. I have a strong preference for the chocolate and marshmallow variety of Pop Tart, so I am not even ingesting whatever microscopic nutrients might be found in the simulated-fruit kind.

"Well, I am very glad to hear that you've been eating a nutritious diet. What about other areas of your life? Are you healthy in other ways?"

I am cognizant of the fact that she is alluding to my drug use, but I have decided to play it coy. Being that I am sitting in a probation meeting, performing the part of a reputable young lady, I choose to pretend that my mind requires more of a prompt to even think of drugs.

"Well, if I'm honest, I could probably stand to exercise more—" I begin.

She smiles. "No, no, Jane, sweetie. I meant are you using anything?"

"Oh." I pretend to be astounded by this question. "No, of course not. Well, besides what I've been prescribed."

She looks down at her tablet. "So, that would be Lithium, Fluvoxamine, and Clozapine?"

I nod.

"Have you been taking anything else?"

"Of course—" I cough "—not."

***

"Hello my name is Selma."
They hang up.
"Hello my name is Phoebe."
They hang up.
"Hello my name is Ann."
They hang up.
"Hello my name is Faith."
They hang up.
"Hello my name is Lillian."
They hang up.
"Hello my name is Sunny."
They hang up.
"Hello my name is Sally."
They hang up.
"Hello my name is Estelle."
They hang up.
"Hello my name is Gertrude."
They hang up.

***

Out of breath from scaling ten floors of stairs and overindulging in twenty-one cigarettes this afternoon, I unlock my apartment door feeling fatigued.

I enter my apartment just in time to witness Keats casually sauntering out of my bedroom.

I am exhausted from a long day of being hung up on. I keep seeing small black blotches floating aimlessly in my field of vision, and there is a dull, tense ache pulsating in my temples. I wanted to come home and sleep. I have been picturing my pillows in the same sort of way that people might fantasise about food or sexual partners. Assaulting Keats was not on my agenda for this evening, and yet here we are.

"What were you doing in my room?" I confront him loudly.

He stops in his tracks and turns towards me.

"I wasn't in your room," he lies.

"What were you doing in my room?" I repeat, louder this time. Benevolently offering him the opportunity to overwrite his lie.

He sputters. "What an accusation, Jane! What is your problem, anyways? What the hell is your deal, anyways? To suggest that I would invade your privacy like that!"

I heave past him, shoving him sideways into the hall closet.

My carpet has Keats-sized foot prints in it and my drawers are all open.

I try to tame what is angry inside of me but it rustles and I twitch.

"Stay the fuck out of my room, Keats!" I begin to yell.

"Stay the FUCK out!"

"Stay the FUCK OUT!"

"STAY THE FUCK OUT!"

***

Keats and I are exchanging pained expressions through the hole that I punched through the plaster wall that separates our bedrooms.

"I think that you may have overreacted," he comments under his breath.

I do occasionally overreact.

***

The pain from my bruised knuckles interrupts my sleep. I spend the night in a strange state somewhere between being awake and dreaming. I see images of bathtubs filled with red water and pills that taste like strawberry liquorice. I am convinced I can make my window shrink with my mind. I feel like I can control the shadows on my bedroom walls.

I watch myself climb out of my bed and light a cigarette. Behind me, I see the shadow of a corner store. I turn around and go inside.

In the morning my mouth tastes sweet and dirty.

***

"Hello my name is Sabrina. I am calling on behalf of—"
They hang up.
"Hello my name is Zelda. I am calling on behalf of—"
They hang up.
"Hello my name is Hilda. I am calling on behalf of—"
They hang up.

***

I have three missed calls on my cell-phone and it is ringing again.

"Hello?" Every time I answer I am greeted with silence. This is becoming increasingly frustrating because my telemarketer's paycheque does not afford me the luxury of having caller I.D. Every time I answer a voiceless call I am aggravated by both the silence and the forced reminder that I am pathetically dispossessed.

***

"Your phone keeps ringing." Keats tosses it into my lap.
"Hello?"
Nothing.

***

Ring. Ring. Ring.
"Yes?"
Nobody.

***

"I need to quit smoking," I lament.
Keats and I have been standing in silence on our balcony for the past twenty-five minutes. He's been sighing the entire time, massaging his forehead and leaning pathetically on the railing. The not-so-picturesque view of off-white high-rises, parking lots filled with broken-down cars and overflowing dumpsters, coupled with Keats' persistent exhalations is creating an excessively bleak atmosphere. Concerned that the depressing environment might prompt Keats to lean all the way off the balcony, I have chosen to start a conversation.
"Why?" He scowls at me irritably.
"I don't know," I shrug, "because of cancer I guess."
He chuckles condescendingly. "Cigarettes won't give you cancer, Jane. The government just wants you to think that everything you enjoy kills you."
"Ah. Is that so?"

He nods. "Yes. It's all done to ensure that we all go to our office jobs, sit in our office cubicles, and live out our pathetic office lives as miserably as possible."

Keats has an odd resentment for offices for someone who has never worked in one.

"But why would they care if we like smoking?" For some inexplicable reason I am possessed to egg him on.

"Oh, shall I count the ways?" he scoffs.

Though I am glad that he has stopped sighing, I would rather die of cancer than hear him do this, so I say, "No."

"No."

Despite this clear and coherent response, I am nonetheless treated to an exhaustive list of the things that the government has withheld from us solely in order to perpetuate our misery. Among the many things listed are marijuana, prostitution, cocaine, polygamy, pitbull puppies and gladiator fighting.

A few minutes into his seemingly endless homily on the ways in which our government has unjustly undercut us, my phone rings.

"Oh gosh, excuse me Keats," I interject. "I am so sorry, but I have just got to take this extremely important phone call."

He pauses in the midst of a sentence apparently involving the word "politicking".

"I absolutely cannot miss this call," I lie, inching away from him and ducking into the apartment.

"Hello?"

Nothing.

"Hellooo? Anybody there?"

Nobody.

***

I came into work this morning to discover a brand-new pen waiting for me at my desk. This pen is also decorated with the words "Larry's Famous Pet Store"; however, this time, the cap is shaped like a little bird.

As I examine the pen, my co-worker Allyssa says, "Getting a lot of gifts from that disabled guy."

I turn to look at her.

"Are you jealous?" I ask loudly.

She rolls her eyes.

"Can't stand seeing someone else getting pens?"

She rolls her eyes again.

"I'll put in a good word for you with Frank," I say, "I'm sure he'd throw a pen your way, Allyssa."

***

"Hello, my name is Alice. I am calling—"

They hang up.

"Hello, my name is Heidi. I am calling—"

They hang up.

"Hello, this is Matilda. I am calling—"

They hang up.

"Hello my name is Harriet. I am calling—"

They hang up.

***

After my lunch break this afternoon, heroin-face touched my arm and said, "I've got you something, if you're into it."

Regular face went inside.

"What?" I asked.

She fished around in her pockets and drew out a smattering of mauve pills with ladybugs carved into them. Being a fan of both winged insects and narcotics, I graciously held out my hand like a child trick-or-treating. Like a churchgoer at communion.

Ivy, Keats, and I took them about forty minutes ago. So far nothing.

"I've never done this before," Ivy confesses.

"Hey, do you feel it?" She starts grinning.

"Oh my God, guys. Do you feel it?"

***

We ride the elevator downward. It produces a worrying mechanical screeching sound as it descends. It moves erratically, as though it is held only by a progressively disintegrating cord of rope.

Keats has his back pressed up against the wall. His eyes are closed. He is gripping the metal handlebar in the elevator so tightly that his fingers are white, and his veins are swollen and visible.

"This isn't safe," he keeps saying.

"This is not safe."

"Do you girls think that this thing is safe?"

When the elevator reaches the ground floor he exits quickly, pushing us aside.

***

We are running.

Sprinting to the bar.

Screaming.

"Do you lie to me a lot?" Keats asks me. The skin on his face is melting.

I laugh.

***

The loud music is making my ribcage rattle. Each of my bones feels like it has its own individual bone-heartbeat, and all of them seem to be engaged in their own miniature cardiac arrests. Keats and Ivy are aggressively making out on the dance floor. I am sitting apathetic at the bar, running my finger over the rim of my glass. The lights are flashing in a way that makes everything look like it is moving in slow motion. Black. Ivy and Keats making out. Black. Ivy and Keats laughing. Black.

Anyone looking at me would see: black, my deadpan face, black, my deadpan face again, black, no change.

I resolve to leave.

As I begin to step out of the bars' front door, ready to make a break for it, an enormous security guard reaches out and touches my arm. "Are you going home alone?" he asks me, his voice loud enough to be heard over the booming music.

"Uh," I reply, eloquently.

"Can I call you a cab?" He eyes me up and down. "You're a small girl. I don't want to see you get hurt."

"I am not that small a girl."

"I've seen girls bigger than you get themselves into trouble."

My ribcage is still vibrating.

"Thank you for your concern," I turn away from him, vaulting myself off the front step, "but I am going to take my chances."

***

I am dissolving a ladybug pill beneath my tongue to liven up my walk home. The trees alongside the road have grown gnarly human hands, and their fingers are all reaching out at me. The road is a black ocean and the cars are sharks who want to eat me. Not today though, sharks and trees! I am not that small a girl!

***

My phone rings.

"Hello?"

"Hello Jane, this is Cindy," my probation counselor says.

"Oh, hi there Cindy."

"I'm just calling to let you know that we're being asked to do surprise home visits now. I'm calling all of my patients to give them a general heads-up. I can't tell you exactly when I'm coming, but I want you to be aware that I will be showing up at your apartment at some point in the near future. Do you understand?"

"Okay thank you," I reply while chewing on a ladybug pill.

"It could be at any time, okay Jane?" she warns me.

"Okay thank you."

My tongue is numb.

"Do you understand?"

"Okay thank you."

***

"Hello my name is Molly."

They hang up.

"Hello my name is Mary-Jane."

They hang up.

"Hello my name is Lucy."

They hang up.

"Hello my name is Charlie."

They hang up.

***

I am dissolving a ladybug pill on the roof of my mouth. It has adhered itself to my palate and is steadily melting. It tastes bitter like rusty metal and uncoated Tylenol.

"Have you ever had an abortion?" Keats asks me through a mouthful of grapes.

"No," I reply, taking a grape from his bowl. "Why, have you?"

The combination of pills and grapes is producing a strange woolly sensation in my mouth.

He smirks. "Yeah. I just can't keep this womanly womb of mine empty."

"Have any of your girlfriends ever had an abortion?"

"Not that I'm aware of." He pops four grapes into his mouth in quick succession. "But that's one of the luxuries of being a man, isn't it? God only knows what offspring I have out in the world, or have avoided having out in the world."

"That's true." I chew. "That is a sort of luxury."

"Ivy's had one." he tells me in a dark, sombre tone, "It was with a different guy."

"Oh yeah?" I pretend that this information is new to me.

"Yeah," he says, chewing loudly.

"Is that something that bothers you?"

He tilts his head. "You know that everything bothers me, Jane."

We chew in rhythm with each other.

"So you've really never had one?" he asks me again.

"Nope," I reply.

***

"Hello my name is Betty."
"Hello my name is Veronica."
"Hello my name is Geraldine—"
"Stop fucking calling me!"
"Hello my name is Midge—"

***

Ivy's father has picked up the phone and interrupted a conversation that she is having at me.

"Ivy?" his voice intersects with hers.

She had been telling me the story of when she bought her first training bra. I consequently welcome the interruption, as the details of a purchase that she made ten years ago have not been delighting me.

"Dad?" She pauses. "Oh my God, Dad. Hang up!"

"You won't believe the car that came in today, Ivy." He chuckles. "It was a Challenger! And do you know what colour it was?"

"Dad, hang up."

"Pink!" he exclaims, laughing. "Can you believe it?"

"Dad, listen to me—"

"I thought of you when I saw it," he laughs again, "I thought, oh boy, wouldn't Ivy love this?"

"I'm sorry Jane," she apologizes to me.

"Jane?" repeats the man.

"The person who I am on the phone with, Dad," she snarls.

"Oh, hello there Jane!" The happy man addresses me.

"Hello Ivy's dad," I reply politely.

"Ivy's told us all about you!"

"No I haven't!" Ivy speaks quickly, evidently embarrassed to have been caught acknowledging my existence to her family.

"All good things I hope," I say.

"Of course!" The man chuckles loudly. "Ivy has given you a five-star review!"

"Five whole stars, eh Ivy?"

He laughs again. "Our Ivy only has great things to say about you, Jane. That's for sure."

***

The first bra I owned was one that I stole from the top drawer of Mrs. Arwol's dresser. I used to wear it with her high heels and her pink lipstick. I would look at myself in her full-length mirror and pretend that I was a mother and a wife. I remember thinking that I looked so beautiful with lipstick smudged across my teeth and an enormous bra dangling limp and hollow from my childish shoulders. I had managed to get lipstick all over my grubby hands so there were pink fingerprints all over the bra. I panicked and tried to wash it in her sink, but the spots were stains. I had to take it or she might have seen the marks and then she would have known.

***

"Hello my name is Corrina."
They hang up.
"Hello my name is Audrey."
They hang up.
"Hello my name is Gloria."
They hang up.

***

"Hello my name is Elliott. I'm calling on behalf of—"
"Don't you dare say another word," the respondent hisses. "Not another word. Do you hear me, you daft little girl?"
"I am calling on behalf of Krippler Incorporated. Today—"
"Are you deaf, Jane? Is that the issue here?"
"No. Today we are conducting a survey on feline diabetes. Do you or any member of your household own a cat?"
"Do you want to know what I own, Jane? I own a shotgun. What do you think of that?"
"Do you own a cat?"
"You are a despicable woman!" he is screaming, "a contemptible and disgraceful excuse for a human being!"

***

"Did you like that new pen?" Frank asks me.
"I did yes, thank you."
"I got ones shaped like kittens too. Do you like kittens?"
"I love kittens, Frank."

***

"Well, isn't that just a fascinating shirt?" my probation counselor remarks, nodding at my stained dinosaur T-shirt.

"Uh. Thank you," I say in response.

I had nearly forgotten that I had a probation meeting scheduled for this afternoon. I remembered just in time to arrive two minutes late for it. I did not, however, remember in time to dress appropriately. I would not have chosen to wear a dirty T-shirt had I remembered. I would have worn a blouse or a blazer or a stiff dark dress. Something that subtly communicated my ability to blend in as a mild-mannered, law-abiding and proper young lady.

I might have also chosen not to eat two ladybug pills moments before the meeting, but que sera, sera. Sometimes the universe's plan differs from my own. Whatever will be will be.

"I apologize for being late," I say, oddly conscious of the way that the words I say make my lips move.

"Oh, what's two minutes?" She winks at me.

I smile weakly.

I smell like cigarettes.

"Now Jane, you remember our phone call the other day, correct? When I warned you about the home visits that they're having us do now?" She locks her pupils with mine.

"I do, yes."

Her pupils are the size of a pencil eraser.

"It is very important that you keep your home in a state that reflects well on you. Do you understand?"

My pupils are probably the size of a bottle cap.

"Do you understand?" she asks me again.

"I do, yes."

"I know that you've been through a lot." She reaches out and touches my knee. The unanticipated physical contact does not sit well with me. I have to fight an impulse to whip her hand away. "I really want the best for you now, and I would really hate for you to take any steps backwards."

"Thank you," I say, at a volume louder than I intended to.

"I'm really rooting for you."

"Thank you," I say, this time too quietly.

***

I have created a mosaic of crushed pills on the top of my dresser. I am arranging the little anthill dust piles according to their different hues: white, pink and yellow. This is a thing of art, ladies and gentlemen. This is something we should look at with tilted heads and sighs of reverence. The muted colours and coarse texture of the geometric mounds are a picturesque allusion to nothing. If you look closely, you'll notice that these colourful little tart-tasting sand hills are reminiscent of my purpose in life.

***

"Hello my name is Mattie. I am calling on behalf of Krippler Incorporated. Today we are conducting a survey on feline diabetes. Do you, or any member of your household, own a cat?"

The respondent breathes heavily down the phone.

"What are you wearing?" they ask in a moan.

"You're disgusting," I say, "but nothing, you?"

***

"Hello?" I answer my phone.

No response.

"Hello?" I say again, louder this time.

"Hellooo?"

***

"Hello my name is Lo. I am calling on behalf of Krippler Incorporated. Today we are conducting a survey on feline diabetes. Do you or any member of your household own a cat?"

"I am on the do not call list!"

"Please let me assure you that I am not selling any—"

They hang up.

"Hello my name is Lola. I am calling on behalf of—"

They hang up.

"Hello my name is Dolly. I am calling on behalf of—"

They hang up.

"Hello my name is Dolores. I am calling on behalf of—"

They hang up.

"Hello my name is Lolita. I am calling on behalf of Krippler Incorporated. Today—"

"HOW MANY TIMES DO I HAVE TO ASK YOU TO STOP?" the respondent screams immediately. "Do I have to change my phone number? Do I have to change my goddamn name? Is death my only possible escape from you, you intolerable excuse for a girl? Please God tell me what exactly it is that I have to do to make your ceaseless calls end!"

"I'm conducting a survey—"

"Wow. May God have mercy on your forsaken soulless body!"

"On feline diabetes—"

"I hope you are the victim of a gruesome, disfiguring accident!"

"Do you, or any member of your family—"

"Preferably an accident that renders you utterly mute! Or crippled and incapable of dialing my phone number! Or dead!"

"—have a cat?"

He hangs up.

***

"I wonder what you were like as a kid," Ivy muses during yet another one of her dreaded phone calls. "Do you think that we would have been friends?"

I am lying in my bed with my eyes closed.

"Do you ever think about that, Jane? About what someone was like as a kid? I do it all the time. Sometimes when I see an old man on the street I think about how he was a baby once. I think it about homeless people especially. Almost every time I see a homeless guy, I think, your mother was probably so excited to have you when she was pregnant and now you have nowhere to sleep. People probably came to the hospital to meet you as a baby. You had a grandma who probably told her friends about you. You played with blocks and stuff. Do you ever think about things like that?"

"No."

"I bet you were a cute kid," she continues, seeming never to rest for air, "I bet you were funny too. Were you a funny kid?"

"I don't really remember what I was like."

"Come on. You must remember something. Were you cute?"

I'm dozing off.

"I remember the skin surrounding my lips was always stained from eating candy." I yawn. "I remember looking in the mirror, washing my face, and the colour never coming off."

My pupils would connect with my reflected pupils. Red and blue chalky residue caked across flushed cheeks. I had a swollen sore tongue and bags under my eyes. Red dirt under my fingernails.

I would buy candy with change that I'd stolen out of my mother's purse. I remember walking with oxidized, dirt-encrusted change in my clenched fist. I would buy hard white sugar sticks. I would hold the sticks with the same grimy fingers I'd held the quarters in. I would lick the sticks and dip them into pouches of red powdered sugar. I would buy jawbreakers the size of my fist and I would lick them until my tongue was raw.

I wore candy necklaces in my hair like pigtails. Knots of torn hair irritated my skull. I would pull the elastic necklace down from my hair into my mouth and chew off the candies and chew my hair. I remember always having hair in my mouth and always having sugar and spit in my hair.

"Your mouth was always stained?" Ivy sounds shocked. "You weren't always eating candy though, were you?"

"Yeah," I answer her, "I was always eating it."

She laughs. "Well, you were one lucky kid then. My parents would've never let me get away with that."

I remember throwing up rainbows into our dirty pink bathroom sink.

"I guess I was lucky." I yawn, rolling onto my side.

When I ran out of dirty purse change I would sit next to the convenience store and beg the people who walked by me to give me change so I could buy more candy.

"We ate, like, mashed potatoes and pork chops every night," Ivy gripes. "It was really disgusting. My parents, like, practically force-fed us salad."

When I was eleven I was tall enough to pass for a teenager. The gangly convenience store cashier would sell me cigarettes instead of candy if I promised that I would sit with him on his break and kiss him.

"We like never had dessert either," Ivy continues.

***

I used to wear a T-shirt that had a picture of a frog printed on it. The frog was sitting on a lily pad and its tongue was reaching out to catch a cartoon fly. That shirt was made for a toddler. I was thirteen when I wore it so it was very small on me. I had stretched it so the frog's face was distorted and expanded, and the fabric was thin and transparent.

My parents would not buy me clothes. I had to steal the unwanted and unwashed clothes from my elementary school lost-and-found box. I also remember trespassing in backyards, tugging things off clotheslines. My wardrobe was an eclectic mishmash of clothes, none of which were designed for my gender, weight, or age. I usually wore boy's gym shorts paired with a large, adult-sized T-Shirt.

When sporting the stolen hand-me-downs of my neighbours and classmates became too degrading for my adolescent pride, I took up shoplifting.

"You are going to get yourself into a lot of trouble one day, little lady," a fat security guard warned me, after catching me elbowing some expensive skinny jeans into my knapsack. "You are a pretty little thing and all, but that isn't always going to get you out of trouble. Do you understand that?"

I remember biting my bottom lip and nodding while fidgeting with the bottom of my frog shirt, intentionally exposing a few inches of abdomen.

I said, "I know, sir. I promise that I won't do it again."

"Okay honey, this time I'll let you go then."

***

The same fat security guard said "You've been caught pinching clothes here before, haven't ya?" when he caught me attempting to shove a sweatshirt into my bag.

"Yes."

"Do you remember how I let you go last time?"

"Yes."

"It isn't always going to be that easy to get out of trouble. Do you know that, honey?"

I bit my bottom lip and nodded, tugging the frog shirt down to expose the freckled skin on my fresh, girlish shoulder.

He smiled at me. "Are you gunna remember what a nice guy I've been to you when you're a couple years older?"

***

Once, the convenience store cashier refused to sell me cigarettes until I promised to sleep over at his house.

He held out a pack of cigarettes for me to take. When I reached out to grab them he pulled them away.

"Not so fast!" He dangled them out of my reach.

"Hey, give me those!" I demanded, unimpressed.

"No. Not until you promise that you'll sleep over at my house tonight."

"Why? I don't want to sleep over at your house."

"Come on."

Despite not really liking him, I did really like cigarettes, so I was forced to begrudgingly accept his solicitation.

"Fine, just give me the cigarettes," I said. At this point in my childhood I had already developed a pretty commanding dependence on nicotine. The prospect of going without it felt even more objectionable than sleeping with this homely cashier.

"I'm going on a sleepover tonight, mom," I informed my mom.

"Okay," she said, but I could tell that she was not really listening to me.

"It's at my friend Sarah's house," I lied, despite knowing that she did not really care where I slept. "She has blonde hair and she plays the violin and—"

"I'm trying to watch the TV," she snapped.

"Sarah's mother doesn't watch TV."

"Who the fuck is Sarah?"

"The girl whose house I'm sleeping over at—"

"Did you not just hear me tell you to shut up? I'm watching the TV."

***

I watched the convenience store cashier play videogames in his basement all night. I sat chain-smoking beside him, bored out of my mind.

He would stop playing periodically to say something along the lines of, "You are kind of hot, do you know that?"

"Thanks."

Then he would thrust his grimy mouth over mine for a few fairy-tale-like moments of disgusting, over-eager groping.

I noticed that he was neither confident nor experienced enough to initiate much beyond the occasional face-plant. I was so bored of watching him play videogames that I was grateful for these brief and nauseating interludes simply because they broke up the time.

I had previously thought of the cashier as being in more control than I was. He was older than me, and he was the one who gave me cigarettes. I thought that he had some sort of authority over me. I noticed in that basement, however, that he was tense when he leaned in to kiss me, and that when I touched his waist it made his palms clammy and his voice break. Because of this, I decided to put my hand down the front of his shorts. This was an experiment, in the interest of science. I wanted to see how he would react.

He pulled away. He was laughing and visibly anxious. I tugged him closer and pushed my hand all the way down his pants, watching his face the whole time.

After that night, I would walk behind the convenience store counter, help myself to cigarettes, and leave the store without paying. I would open bags of candy just to eat one piece. I would wink at the cashier as I left the store, arrogantly gnawing on my embezzled candy. I was Queen of the Corner Store.

I fell asleep next to him that night in the basement. I remember my mouth tasting fuzzy and dirty, and I remember him spooning my back. The next morning I was awake before him, but I did not get up. I stayed still, staring at the exposed pipes in the ceiling above me.

I sat up, afraid, when I heard the basement door open and the sound of feet on the stairs.

The cashier's father reached the bottom of the staircase and looked across the room at us. My eyes connected with his and I braced myself to be yelled at, thrown out of their house, or hit.

To my surprise, he grinned at me. He walked over, looked down at his bleary-eyed offspring, then rustled his son's hair in a happy display of fatherly pride.

"Atta boy, convenience store cashier," he said, except he used the boy's actual name (which I now forget).

He said, "That's my son, alright."

He then looked me over and winked.

I smiled assertively back at him, and saw in his blushing features a shy nervousness that mirrored his son's. I was Queen of the Basement.

***

"Are you ready to talk to me about your childhood now?" My probation counsellor asks me.

I was unaware that I had ever given her the impression that I needed to be "ready" to talk to her about that.

"Yes sure." I nod, gulping down a sip of the bitter tea that she's served me.

I am sitting in her office with my legs crossed, wearing a modest black dress, sipping camomile tea from a dainty white cup. When my counsellor asked me how I took my tea I lied. I usually take two sugars, this has none. I lied in order to avoid troubling her. Now I have to swig down this sour poison-water, as well as stifle the sickened expressions my face keeps attempting to make when I taste it.

"What would you like to know about my childhood?" I ask her, contorting my face in an attempt to transform my tea-grimace into an innocent smile.

"Well, my understanding is that you had a pretty damaging childhood," she says delicately, as if the gentle tone of her voice will somehow soften that reality.

I sip from my tea-cup again. I am trying to ingest the full cup as quickly as possible so I do not have to endure the experience of drinking it any longer than necessary.

"Do you feel like your upbringing has had a negative impact on your life now as an adult?"

"Yes," I answer immediately, without putting any thought into how she will interpret that response.

I clear my throat. "Well, I mean, yes of course it has."

She looks at my empty cup and says obligingly, "Oh, are you finished with your tea, honey? Let me get you some more."

I grit my back molars together and say, "Oh, thank you."

***

"Hello my name is Maggie, I'm calling on behalf of Krippler Incorporated—"

"You're what?" An old man with a throaty smoker's voice replies to me.

"I'm calling on behalf of—"

"Speak up!"

"I'm calling on behalf of—"

"What?"

"Krippler Incorporated."

"Are you trying to sell me something?" He coughs.

"No, today I'm conducting a survey—"

"You're what?"

***

"You know, I been collecting pens for 'bout forty years," Frank shares with me.

He is keeping me company outside while I smoke. Despite it being minus thirty, Frank has generously opted to stand in the snowy back alley with me.

I manage to light my cigarette after three failed attempts.

"Oh, yeah?" I inhale. "So why do you collect pens anyways? Why not collect something else?"

"I dunno, I just really like pens, to be honest with you. They just look really good to me."

I take another puff.

The hand I am using to hold my cigarette is freezing cold and becoming increasingly numb.

"I don't collect anything," I comment while passing my cigarette to my other hand and shoving the freezing one into my coat pocket.

"Well, maybe you should," Frank suggests.

"Why? What's the point?" I ask while struggling to hold the cigarette properly in my less dominant hand.

"Well," he says, crossing his arms, "if I didn't collect any pens then I wouldn't a been able to give you any pens. See?"

"I see. I guess that is true."

"Right." He nods knowledgeably. "And then I wouldn't have got anything to repay you with."

"You don't have to repay me for anything, Frank," I say while accidently dropping my cigarette into the fluffy grey snow.

***

Ivy has expressed concern that our apartment fails to meet her jovial requirements for the festive season. Because of this, she, Keats, and I are now shopping for Christmas decorations.

Though I am not personally troubled by the cheerless ambiance of our apartment, I agreed to shop in order to appease her. Keats, on the other hand, had to be dragged.

He is irritated at the suggestion that we comply with the "corporate commercialization of a sacred religious holiday," and he has been discussing his reservations at length.

"A home without decorations celebrates Christmas much better than one with materialistic garbage, like Christmas trees," he rambles. "Who in their right mind needs a godforsaken Christmas tree? Do you realize who profits from our Christmas tree purchases? The Russian government. They don't make it obvious, sure, but ask any Christmas tree salesman where his father was born and I can almost guarantee—"

Rather than endure another instant of Keats' illogical ranting, I try to interrupt him.

"Aren't you an atheist, Keats? One who's voiced his major qualms about Christianity to me, despite my expressed lack of interest? Maybe undermining the meaning of Christmas would be an excellent way for you to contest the Christian faith?"

He splutters. "Yeah, well, I mean, I guess."

Despite my efforts to stop Keats from talking, he revs back up within moments.

"Are you two aware of the biochemical ingredients used to produce Christmas lights?" he says, earnestly, "It's astounding that the purchasing public would so ignorantly continue to support the production of…"

He blathers on until all language ceases to have meaning and my ears involuntarily begin to deafen themselves and melt into my skull.

I tune him out, gawking lifelessly down into our shopping cart.

So far, the shopping cart contains: a small nativity scene of anthropomorphic cats, a selection of Christmas themed shot glasses, and an artful, ceramic statue of Rudolf looking dejected.

I scan the store we're shopping in while Keats' mouth continues to open and close, open and close, open and close. This draws my attention to a teenage boy standing a little way away who keeps staring at me.

Keats is still rambling. He is now explaining why he refuses to go to his parents' town for Christmas. It seems that he thinks that the mayor there is involved in some elaborate undercover KKK movement, and he resents his family for not taking his concerns about this more seriously.

"Yeah, I'm going to go spend Christmas in a community of undercover racist psychopaths," he says under his breath, "sounds real merry. They'll probably have banners in the streets wishing everyone a happy white Christmas. Everyone will be totally ignorant to the sick double-meaning."

I nod along to his nonsensical tirade while I examine a package of root beer flavoured candy canes, trying vainly to ignore the teenager who I can sense is still staring at me.

"My mom expects me to come, and what? Sing carols to a community in the beginning stages of fascism, like some sort of pre-war Nazi Germany? Yeah right, mom," Keats snorts. "I'll get right on that."

"Why do they make candy canes like this?" I interrupt him, hopeful that a shift in topic will put an end to this unsolicited sermon.

Rather than acknowledge my question, Ivy chimes in with her own thoughts.

She asks me, "Why aren't you going anywhere for Christmas, Jane? Because of your parents being dead?"

I nod, still examining the candy canes.

Keats glares at Ivy and whispers unpleasantly, "Well, that was pretty insensitive, Ivy. Couldn't you have worded that a little more delicately—"

"Don't you have, like, grandparents or something?" Ivy asks me, ignoring him.

I nod. "Yeah I do, but." I pause. "But I don't know. I don't really feel like participating in all of the stupid commercialization, do you know what I mean?" I deliberately pander to Keats' interests to stave Ivy off.

Keats' eyes widen in agreement. He nods passionately. "Yeah, don't even get me started. Christmas is the celebration of Jesus' birth, you say? More like the celebration of Walmart." He laughs loudly. "Ha!" He shakes his head and repeats, "Ha!" for emphasis.

He then begins to discuss slave labour and the deplorable wages of Walmart employees.

"Don't even get me started," he says, despite having already started, "don't even get me started."

As I begin to tune Keats out again, I turn to check if that teenager is still looking at me.

As I turn, I see him quickly look away from me, demonstrating that he had in fact still been staring at me. Annoyed by this, I resolve to confront him.

"Hey. What do you want?" I shout at him.

His face immediately flushes pink.

"Oh. Hi," he says.

I narrow my eyes.

"Hi, um, I think you used to babysit me..." He laughs unevenly.

"Oh." I open my mouth, suddenly recognizing him as being Timothy Arwol. Once a handsome child, he has evolved into the slender, gawky version of his ugly father.

"Timmy," I say. "You've grown."

He forces a pained grin, revealing teeth adorned with multi-coloured metal braces.

"Yeah, a bit. Yeah," his eyes dart to his feet.

I scrutinize his entire person without any restraint. His Superman T-shirt falls from boney shoulders, across a hollow chest. He has acne on the sides of his neck and a blonde, puerile moustache athwart his upper lip. He has arms that hang like a chimp's, and the overall lumbering and apprehensive air of a person who recently grew a lot in a short space of time.

He shifts his weight from one foot to the other.

"Don't tell my parents that I saw you," he says quickly, his rapid mumbling almost impossible to decipher.

I chew on the insides of my mouth.

I nod. "I never talk to them."

He laughs loudly. "Yeah. Yeah I know that. I guess that was a pretty stupid thing of me to say. I'm sorry."

"No no." I shake my head. "I get it. It is weird."

His face is now bright red.

"I shouldn't have said hi," he says under his breath.

"You didn't really," I say, tasting my own blood inside of my mouth. I have gnawed my inner cheeks raw. "You just saw me and I approached you. We can both just forget about it."

"Yeah," he laughs strangely, scratching the back of his neck.

"It was nice to see you," I say sharply, ending the interaction.

"Yeah," he looks at his feet, "yeah."

After he leaves the aisle, I tell Ivy and Keats that I am going to wait for them outside.

I then lumber unstably towards the exit.

***

I leave the store overwhelmingly nauseous.

I trudge around to the back of the building, attempting to avoid the people in the parking lot, and to possibly puke in private. Behind the building, however, I find myself in a quiet neighbourhood park.

There is a kid doing cartwheels in the snow. Her parents are sitting on a bench and watching her. Both parents are drinking out of takeout coffee cups and they are holding each other's hands.

"Watch me mom!"

"Watch me dad!"

"Watch me! Watch me! Watch me!"

Her father moves his arm to sit on her mother's shoulder.

"Watch me!"

The mother leans her head to rest on the father's chest.

"Watch me!"

I feel really angry.

***

Ivy was forced to work at her parents' car wash today. She was quite vocal about not wanting to do this. She referred to going to work as "torture".

"I hate the car wash," she whined, her head flung back.

"It's torture!"

Though I can certainly commiserate with hating one's work, I find her baseless animosity for her family's lucrative business kind of off-putting and bratty. Perhaps she has some sixth sense however, and knew that going to work today was a bad idea. This is because during her shift today she managed to sustain a Workplace Injury.

She got her leg wedged in some car washing apparatus, and has injured both her foot and her ankle. Her foot in particular is badly cut.

"I hate that fucking car wash," she groans from the couch, twisting her body gawkily in an attempt to ease the pain. "I hate it so much."

Keats tries to comfort her by saying pacifyingly, "Maybe you'll get a cool scar."

She frowns at him, apparently un-consoled by the prospect of having a long-lasting imperfection on her otherwise perfect foot.

"Scars are cool, Ivy," he explains to her. "They add character."

Her phone keeps ringing.

She looks down at it and groans. "Ugh. It's my mom." She rolls her eyes melodramatically, ignoring the call. "She keeps asking me how my foot is. Like, oh my God mom, it hasn't changed in the past ten minutes."

Keats lifts his T-shirt to unveil a thin scar ploughed across his pale, unsightly chest.

"I mean just look at this scar!" he exclaims. "I got it falling out of a tree! I used to climb the trees near my parents' house all the time, you know. I got to the very top of a ten-story pine tree once, honest to God. To the very top!"

Ivy's lifeless, scowling expression suggests that Keats efforts to comfort her are still failing.

"Come on Jane!" He hits the side of my leg. "Show Ivy a cool scar you've got!"

Though I am aware that this scar themed show-and-tell is not helping Ivy, I pull my pant legs up to share some scars that I like on my knees.

"How'd you get them?" Keats asks, leaning in to get a good look.

He, for whatever contemptible reason, has not yet put his shirt back on.

"Playing hockey," I lie. "You know, falling on the ice and stuff."

"See!" Keats grins at Ivy. "Do you see that, Ivy? I would have never known Jane even played hockey if I hadn't seen those scars! Do you see that?"

***

My parents collected scrap and kept it heaped in our yard. I spent a lot of my time running around that yard, ducking through masses of junk.

My dad habitually sat on the back porch, shooting the racoons that he saw diving behind his scrap-piles. While I was playing, I often worried that he might mistake me for a racoon. This fear elicited a rush of endorphins that exhilarated me and made playing in the yard a lot more exciting. It was clear even then that I would make a promising drug addict.

I was wearing pale pink socks that had lace borders around the ankles. The ground was wet and the soles of my socks were soggy and dirty. I had a mason jar with a hole in the lid that I sucked through, filled with what I thought was special juice that my mother hid in her closet from me.

I was spinning around in circles, imagining that I was a rabid racoon. I rubbed dirt into my eye sockets to mimic a racoon's mask. I crawled around on my knees through dirt that was mixed with powdered, shattered glass.

In a brief moment of lucidity, I realized that I was badly cut on my knees and face. The pain receptors in my body sent a delayed message to my brain. I was hurt.

I ran next door to the Arwol's house to tell them that I needed help.

Mrs. Arwol answered the door. She led me by the hand into her kitchen, picked me up, and put me on the kitchen counter. I sat swinging my lacerated legs. She put alcohol and Band-Aids on me, and kissed both of my knees.

When she was done she said, "Alright honey, I think you're going to make it."

***

"Hello?" I answer my phone.
No one replies.
"Hello?"
Nothing.

***

It is 1:00 a.m. and my phone is ringing again.
"Hello?" I croak.
No one answers.
"Who is this?" I grumble, tired.
Nothing.

***

I am once again torn from sleep by the irritating buzz of my phone.
"Hello?" I hold my breath.
To my surprise, someone replies.
"Hi!"
"Who is this?" I ask, sitting up slightly.
"Ivy!"
"Oh." I exhale, lying back down.
"Come to the bar!" she petitions me.
"Uh, no thanks," I reply groggily.
"Please! Come on!"
"No thanks," I say again, preparing now to hang up.
"Come on! I'll buy you a drink!"

"A drink? Okay then. Alright."

∗∗∗

I enter the booming, muggy bar and immediately begin scanning the area for Ivy. While doing so I assess the clientele. I resolve that I am not impressed by the bar's population of out-of-it underage girls. Not interested in spending any more time in this establishment than necessary, I shove my way through the crowd of soon-to-be mothers until I find Ivy. She and a bearded man who has a large tattoo of a dog emblazoned forever on his bicep are pirouetting together.

When Ivy sees me she grabs the man's arm and begins dragging him towards me.

"Jane! This is Brian!" she shouts at me, grinning manically.

"Who?"

"Brian!" she repeats.

Brian smiles weakly at me.

Ivy grins frenziedly at me and then disappears into the hazy crowd like a malevolent necromancer.

"So, I'm Brian!" Brian shouts into my ear.

Ivy had promised to buy me a drink. I accepted her invitation to this bar solely to accept that drink and then to leave. I got out of my comfortable bed, I put on uncomfortable pants, and I walked here. I am realizing now that I was cheated into coming here to meet this man whose name appears to be Brian. Ivy has been possessed to set me up. She is deluded enough to assume that I could feel romantically for a person with a badly drawn dog tattooed to their arm. In reality I suspect that I am incapable of feeling romantically for any, even normal, person.

I therefore feel too sullen and betrayed to engage with this "Brian", despite his being entirely blameless in this. I do not respond to him when he speaks, and instead cross my arms and stare forwards.

"And your name is Jane?" Brian shouts, ejecting his hot breath into my unconsenting ear.

I scan the dance floor for Ivy but can't spot her.

After accepting that Ivy is gone, I try to shake Brian off by escaping to the women's washroom. I weave through the crowd until I think that I've lost him.

I enter the bathroom, irritated. I walk past the gaggle of girls applying makeup at the mirrors, throw open a stall, and use the top of the toilet-roll dispenser and my credit card to crush two pills into an ingestible dust.

***

I leave the bathroom and almost crash into Brian, who is standing just outside of the door. He has been waiting for me. I twist my eyebrows at him in an effort to communicate nonverbally how creepy I find his waiting for me.

Apparently unable to decrypt my silent facial cues, he smiles at me.

"I heard Ivy offer to buy you a drink when she called you," he grins, "I'll get you that drink, okay?"

I untwist my eyebrows and nod. Despite my trepidations about Brian's possible intention to poison me, I would like a free drink.

"What would you like to drink?" he asks me.

"Whatever is cheapest." I shrug, having no real preferences besides a high alcohol content.

"So you're a cheap date?" He smiles at me again.

I fake friendliness with a smile.

"Are we on a date?" I ask.

He laughs. "Well, we could be. You're a pretty good-looking girl."

I suppress my instinct to cringe. I find almost all forms of flirting intensely embarrassing.

"Thanks. I am a pretty cheap date." I circle back to his original question.

He orders me a large rum and coke.

I take the drink directly from the bartender, position the straw in my mouth, and lean back on the bar.

I look into Brian's eyes while moving the straw over my lips. "I'm a really, really easy, cheap date," I say, sucking through the straw and then winking.

Despite finding flirting humiliating I have successfully mastered the skill.

Brian laughs sheepishly at me. "Wow."

I leave the bar immediately after finishing the drink.

***

I think that the skin on my thighs is infected. I carved the alphabet in a circle around my leg, in the same area that a garter would sit. Letters H through P are excreting white blood cells like they're confetti and it is midnight, New Year's Eve, 1999, at a party hosted by the CEO of a confetti plant.

***

"Hello my name is Chelsea."
They hang up.
"Hello my name is Kathleen."
They hang up.
"Hello my name is Krista."
They hang up.

***

"C'I bum a smoke?" heroin-face asks me in the alley behind the office.

I hand her one reluctantly.

"Thanks," she takes it and attempts to light it, "I meant to ask you, did you have a good time with those ladybug capsules, baby?"

I am uncomfortable with her calling me "baby", as I am neither an infant nor romantically involved with her. Despite my discomfort, I reply, "Yes I did thank you," because I am respectful of those with substance dependencies, and because I am inclined to demonstrate particular reverence for those who distribute such substances to me.

"You're a party girl, eh?" She rolls her thin lips back, revealing teeth that remind me of buttered popcorn.

I tut. "Yeah, I guess. Sure."

"Want to come to a party tonight with me then, baby?" She grins demonically.

I am yet again troubled by my new pet name. I did, however, enjoy the ladybug pills, and to decline an invitation to potentially consume more would feel imprudent.

"Is it a ladybug party?" I investigate with caution.

"It can be." She nods.

I shrug. "Yeah, sure."

***

Heroin-face lives in a wood paneled basement. If she ever moves out I would wager that her landlord will not be returning her security deposit. Her drug use, coupled with her ownership of what must be a small herd of cats, has been hard on this quaint bachelor.

Perhaps I am being overly critical. Perhaps the accommodation was in disrepair when she moved in. It could be that my standard of living has been more privileged than I had previously realized. Maybe this affable addict cannot afford to live in a home that isn't an opium den, and who am I judge her for that?

Her bed is a mattress on the ground with no sheet. There's cat litter heaped in a corner, without a box to house it. The carpet appears to be shag but this is possibly an illusion brought about by at least three seasons of cat hair shedding. The atmosphere is further enhanced by the appetizing smell of stale cigarette smoke and cat piss.

A black cat is sitting on my lap. I can feel his ribcage when I pet him.

"This cat is a bit thin," I point out to her.

She looks at him. "Yeah, he's a picky eater, that one."

All of the cats here are thin though, and while I am no detective or veterinarian I suspect that the cause is less to do with a finicky diet and more to do with a scarcity of food.

"Got any Fancy Feast?"

"What?"

"Do you have a can of tuna or something?"

"Nah, I gotta grocery shop," she says.

The emaciated cat nuzzles his sad head on my jaw.

"Can I you get a glass of water or something?" she offers me warmly.

"No." I reject her offer without sensitivity, as I am both nauseated by the prospect of drinking from one her grimy cups and bothered by her treatment of this dying, amiable cat.

"When's the party?" I ask.

"We'll make it." She winks at me.

"We'll make it?" I repeat, confused. "Where are the ladybugs?"

"Hold your horses," she says. "You gotta meet Donnie first."

"Who's Donnie?"

"Donnie's got the ladybugs. He's got all sorts of bugs." She winks at me once again and laughs.

I laugh along uncomfortably with her even though Donnie's collection of bugs sounds less endearing than it does catching.

***

As it turns out, my acceptance of the heroin addict's invitation to party may have been a case of poor judgement.

Donnie has arrived home. He is the oily archetype of a mob boss.

"Who's this?" Al Capone asks, nodding at me.

"This is Jane, ain't she a cute girl?" Heroin-face winks at me again.

"I'm flattered," I lie.

Donnie looks at me as though he is inspecting a portion of decaying salami.

"Yeah, she's alright," he grunts.

"Oh stop." I wave my hand, feeling mildly slighted. Why doesn't the oily man like me?

"What's she doing here anyways?" he asks gutturally.

"She's into beetles baby," says heroin-face.

"She into paying for beetles?" Donnie asks, still staring at me.

"I can pay for the pills," I interpose.

"Yeah baby she can pay, look at her," heroin-face grins, "you can pay right, baby?"

Donnie, perspiring and obese, continues watching me from behind her. He is now adjusting his belt.

"Yeah, I can pay…" I respond slowly.

"Can ya?" heroin-face asks while biting her lip.

"With money…" I clarify cautiously, sensing now that money is not the kind of payment they are referring to.

She giggles. "What if we don't want money, baby?"

"Please don't call me baby anymore."

"Baby," Donnie grunts from behind her hostilely.

He is now unbuttoning his shirt.

Heroin-face smiles at me like some sort of deranged imp. "How can I make you feel more comfortable?"

Why is this happening to me?

"The word more suggests that I am currently experiencing some degree of comfort. This, if you were unsure, is not the case."

"She talks a lot, Haley," says the man, who is now regrettably shirtless.

"Shh." Haley puts her decrepit finger up to my lips.

"I know what'll make you comfy." She grins.
Heroin.

***

She wasn't wrong.

***

The corpulent Italian man does not partake.
In the heroin, that is.
He does partake in the other bit, to my distaste.
The other bit is sex.
I am unfortunately also a participant.
I feel extraordinarily high.
Metaphysically high.
Supernaturally high.
Biblically high.
Psychologically.
Philosophically.
Futuristically.
Theologically.
Technologically.
Geographically.
Celestially.
My limbs are limp and I cannot focus my eyes. I don't really care
what's happening.
Haley is lying motionless beside me. If she were not producing
this loud and off-putting humming sound I might be concerned
that she'd died.
"Hey there sailor," I keep saying. I don't know why.
Haley hums "mmmhmmmmhmmmm."
"Sailor, hey."
"Mmmhmmm."
"Hey sailor."

"Hi ho sailor."
"Sail me away."

***

I leave the wood panelled cat necropolis and enter the wide-open space that is the outdoors.

Upon exiting, I spot a lone brick on the curb. I grab it and I use it to prop Haley's door open.

"Be free, cats," I whisper down the staircase, "escape to the wide-open space that is the outdoors."

***

The bus I am riding on must be on its way to a garbage convention. Never before has a more rancid assemblage of people congregated. I am at this moment privy to a momentous moment in the history of human smell. My name will probably be memorized by future students, preparing to answer this frequently asked exam question:

Who demonstrated a supernatural ability to remain conscious on the most disgusting vehicle to ever disturb our debauched world?

For extra credit, responses to this question should note my impressively high drug tolerance.

I have received seven missed calls, and my phone is buzzing yet again.

I feel like I was hit by a garbage truck, and then thrown into the back of it. One with the rotten banana peels; I am trash.

Because all of the seats on the bus have been taken I am being forced to stand. I am tempted to ball my sweater up and stuff it into my shirt so that I can pretend that I am pregnant and demand priority seating.

My sympathies go out to the bus driver, who is either having a seizure or has just been electrocuted. These are the only reasons

I can perceive for his erratic and unpredictable use of the breaks. I keep losing my footing and falling into the woman in front of me, who might not even be a woman at all. She might very well actually be a mass of decaying compost detained inside a human-shaped bag, considering her capacity for movement or reaction.

My phone is buzzing again. Worried that it is my probation counselor, I decide to answer it.

I am now balancing with one hand gripping the bus-pole, and one hand holding my phone up to my ear.

"Hello?" I say, uneasily. Unable to mask the sound of discontent in my voice.

Someone is touching the back of my thigh. I have, until now, chosen to assume that the touching is unintentional. An accidental invasion of my personal space, due entirely to our shared misfortune. The strength of my conviction is now waning. The touching has persisted for ten minutes and I have just experienced a definite squeezing sensation.

"Get the hell off of me," I bark at the bus pervert.

"Excuse me?" says the man on the other end of the phone.

"Not you, sorry."

"Where are you?" the man on the phone asks me.

"I am in my living room," I lie.

"Good."

Then without any warning he hangs up on me.

You have been duped, stranger on the phone. I am not in my living room at all. I am in the dissolute netherworlds of public transportation. At one with the grimy degenerates of our society. I am the single clean thread in the unhygienic tapestry that is this hellish toilet of a bus.

***

"Thank God you're home!" Keats exhales as soon as I walk through the door.

"Yeah," I breathe, dropping my bag and coat at my feet.

Even though my journey home was wrought with unspeakable turmoil, I have reached my final destination reasonably unscathed.

"Shut the door, shut the door!" Keats shouts at me.

I shut the door.

"What the hell happened to you?" he asks, eyeing me up and down. "You look like you were mugged."

"Thank you," I glare at him.

"Anyways look." He gestures towards a folded piece of paper sitting on the coffee table. "Look at that!" he exclaims again.

Depressed by the atrocities that I have managed to live through today, I cannot even simulate interest in Keats.

"Just take a look at it!" he demands again.

I scowl at him.

"Look!" he screams, picking up the piece of paper and forcing it into my field of vision.

The paper says: Hello Jane.

"Hi Keats…" I squint at him, confused.

"It's not from me, Jane! Come on! It was shoved under our door!"

I take the paper from his hand and examine it.

"Who do you think it's from?" he asks me, his face and voice noticeably panicked.

"Uh. It's probably from my cousin from Illinois…" I lie.

I have no family in Illinois.

"Look at it, Jane. Will you look at it? It doesn't even have a stamp on it! Or any other postal markings!"

"Oh." I turn the note over, examining it further. "That is kind of strange."

"Yeah," he nods frantically, "it is strange. It means that whoever it's from had to come right to our apartment! Right to our door!"

"I too am capable of summarizing the current situation, Keats. Thank you for your briefing though."

He opens his mouth and straightens his head. "Now is not the time for your sarcasm, Jane."

I laugh a little too loudly.

"It's not funny! This is threatening! What are we going to do!" He is yelling now. "Who would do this to us!"

"Calm down," I groan.

"This could be a stalker, Jane! This could be someone monitoring our apartment! This could be the police!"

"I highly doubt that it's the police," I mutter, turning the paper over.

"Do you have any angry ex-boyfriends or anything?" he asks me desperately. "Is there anybody out in the world who would want to harm you?"

"I'm sure it's nothing." I ignore the question.

"Aren't you alarmed by this?" He's shouting now. "Aren't you!"

The truth is that I am moderately troubled by this note; however, I find that exuding distress rarely makes undesirable situations any better. My experiences suggest that it is best to fake composure, even when you feel fear.

"What are you going to do?" Keats probes, his desperate eyes eager.

"I'm going to nap, Keats."

***

"Hello, my name is Patti. I am calling on behalf of—"

They hang up.

"Hello my name is Courtney, I am calling on behalf of Krip—"

They hang up.

"Hello my name is Stevie. I am calling on behalf of Krippler In—"

They hang up.

***

"Hello my name is Bridget. I am calling on behalf of Krippler Incorporated. Today we are conducting a survey on feline diabetes. Do you, or any member of your household, own a cat?"

"Hello there. Yes, I do actually. I've got two lovely cats living over here with me."

"Great. What are their ages?"

"Oh, let's see. Well, I'd say that they're both about four years old now."

"Okay, great. Do they have any health problems?"

"Oh, no. They are both in pretty good shape actually," the woman answers me, sounding chipper. "What about you dear, do you have any cats?"

"Me?" I respond. "Oh, yeah. I have one." I lie.

"Oh, yeah? What's he like?"

"It's a she," I correct her assumptions about my imaginary cat's gender. "She's white and brown with short fur. She's very friendly. Her name is Lou."

"You got kids?" the woman asks. "How does Lou get along with your kids?"

"I do," I lie. "I have one son. They get along well enough. What about you? Do you have any kids?"

"Me? Oh, well, my kids are all grown up now."

"Oh," I say.

"It's nice to get a phone call once in a while," the woman says.

***

Frank and I are standing in line, waiting to buy lunch.

"What will you get??" Frank asks me.

"A piece of cake," I answer him.

After ordering his food, he tells the cashier, "And I'll be getting this girl a piece of cake!"

"Oh Jesus, no Frank, that's okay," I say, trying to stop him.

He hands the cashier his money before I can intercept.

I then sit in the cafeteria shamefully dodging the judgemental glances that the lunch-ladies shoot me for letting a disabled man pay for my food.

***

After one of the customary lulls during a phone conversation with Ivy, she asks me, "When was your first period?"

I grimace. "I don't know, why?"

"I don't know. I just find it interesting to know. How old were you?"

"I am concerned about the things that you find interesting."

"Well, I was nine," she says sharply, apparently offended by my reaction to her poorly selected topic.

Silence.

"Me too," I say, just to fill the horrible quiet.

"That's pretty young."

"Yeah, I guess."

I was really thirteen.

"Tell me the story of how you got it," she requests.

I yawn. "No."

"Okay fine. Well I was in gym class. I had to tell my gym teacher. Can you believe that? She gave me a pad. It was one of those pads that are made for women after they have had babies, I swear. It honestly felt like a diaper. Then, of course, I got a speech about human reproduction. Cringe, am I right?"

I say nothing.

"Your turn," she sings.

"I don't remember."

***

I was not given words about human reproduction. I told my mom that I was bleeding and she provided me with directions to the underbelly of the bathroom sink. Beyond these instructions I was given no information. I was left to sort out my own thoughts about what was happening, assuming quite rationally that I was dying. I assumed that this unlucky experience was some enigmatic plight inflicted upon only me, and that I probably only had days left to live.

***

Two months after my first period, my mom asked me if I needed any "maxi pads." I remember her exact phrasing because it made her uncomfortable. She winced when she said it.

"Do you need any…" she winced, "…maxi pads?"

She was not comfortable discussing anything even mildly associated with sex. I'd hinted once that I needed a bra, and the conversation felt like I was asking her to plan me an orgy.

"Nope! I don't need any of those, thankfully! I don't get that horrific blood problem anymore!" I replied very sprightly, pleased to have recovered from that weird and embarrassing sickness.

Confused by this response, she squinted at me.

"Maybe we should go to the doctor to see if your body is screwed up or something," she said.

I replied, "Yeah okay sure", even though I did not follow why she wanted to go to the doctor now, when my horrific problem had stopped, rather than during the time when I had been dying from it.

***

I was blindsided when the doctor told me that I was pregnant. More blindsided than your typical pregnant thirteen-year-old because I was not familiar with how any women got pregnant to begin with.

***

Privately, the doctor told me about abortion. This was another subject I had yet to learn about.

He said, "Some people don't believe in abortion for religious reasons or because of other personal beliefs, but a lot of women do it."

"Yeah, I'll do that for sure," I breathed, relieved.

Thank you God for abortions, I thought to myself.

Praise Jesus for abortions.

***

Then my mom came into the room.

The doctor sat her down and he told her the same way that he told me.

"It seems Samantha's pregnant."

My mother laughed at first. She laughed a really loud, weird laugh, that slowly degraded into disbelief. After a moment she said, "No. That has to be wrong." Then, louder this time, "What the fuck do you mean? How the fuck is that even possible?"

***

The doctor told my mom about my decision to terminate the pregnancy and my mother said no. The relief I felt upon hearing about abortion dissipated and my horror was reborn.

"Why not, mom?" I whined like I would whine when she wouldn't buy me the chocolate bar I wanted at the grocery checkout.

"Plllllease?"

"Don't even speak to me!" she said without looking at me.

So, just as I had been denied chocolate, I wasn't allowed an abortion.

***

"How did you even get pregnant?" she asked me in the car after a long period of silence. She still wasn't looking at me.

Not familiar with how anyone got pregnant, I answered truthfully.

"I have no idea."

She jeered, "You are a fucking child whore."

"A fucking child whore."

"A fucking child whore."

***

We got home and I ran up the staircase into my bedroom, like I always did when I was in trouble.

I sat cross-legged against my closed door. I pressed my ear up to the crack around the door frame, listening to my parents discussing my punishment.

My mother told my father repeatedly that I was a "fucking child whore."

"That bastard baby is going up for adoption, I'll tell you that much."

"She's lucky we don't put her up for adoption, fucking child whore."

"Fucking child whore."

***

I got pregnant enough to show before I woke up covered in blood, with sharp, stabbing pains in my abdomen.

***

My mom didn't take me to the hospital for hours.

"Did you do this?" she asked me, looking at me in the face for the first time since the doctor's appointment.

I didn't understand what she was asking me.

73

She threw my closet door open and started violently pulling clothes hangers out.

There was a dress on the ground of my closet. It had slipped off a hanger.

She picked it up. "Where's the hanger for this dress, Samantha?"

I had no idea why we were talking about hangers.

I was covered in blood and I was upset that she was yelling at me, so I started to cry.

She interpreted that as some sort of admission of guilt and slapped me.

"What devil is in you?" she screamed as loudly as she was capable of screaming.

"I don't know!" I screamed as loudly as I could back at her.

***

I am once again throwing a blood party for myself and the bathtub. I am letting the water run for longer than I should. It is starting to spill over the acrylic perimeter of the tub. I am cutting planet shapes into my thighs and onto my stomach.

Hello, I am a solar system. I am calling on behalf of the universe. Today we are conducting a survey on moons and asteroids. Do you or any member of your family believe in aliens?

They hang up.

***

"Today I'm conducting a survey on feline—"
"Stop calling me, you insufferable slut!"

***

Heroin-face and I are smoking.

Unhappy to be alone in her presence, I have been imagining that she isn't here. I have not looked at or spoken to her since stepping outside.

"Are you in the market for anything?" she asks me in a hushed voice, after two minutes of silence.

I scowl.

"What do you mean? In the market for what?"

She looks around before reaching into her pocket and pulling out a small clear bag full of white dust.

"Yeah, I'm in the market for that," I say, extending my arm.

"You gotta pay me this time, baby," she taunts, pulling the bag out of my reach.

"I can pay you with money if that's what you want," I say, looking into her worn-out face. Then, very clearly: "If you are asking me for any other form of payment, I'm afraid I'll have to pass this time. Do you understand?"

"Money works," she nods. "It's cool."

"Great," I murmur and reach into my pocket for my wallet.

We make the exchange and return to silence. After a couple of minutes she makes an attempt at friendly small-talk. "It's a nice night," she says.

I don't reply.

***

I absentmindedly dial the number written on my post-it note.

Before I have a chance to speak, the enraged respondent begins to scream at me.

"You are the scum of the earth, Jane! If I ever get my hands on you I SWEAR TO GOD I'LL—"

While he is raging, I notice my line-manager Rick scuttling around the office, whispering into cubicles and looking distressed.

When he reaches my desk, he whispers, "After your call, come to the meeting room, okay?"

"Okay." I nod, and hang up on the still raging man.

**

There are more people than chairs in the meeting room so many of us are standing. Rick is sitting at the front of the room, at the head of the table, like the patriarch at a dinner table.

Someone has a cough and keeps clearing their throat. The fluorescent strip-light is blinking fitfully and the room smells like damp cigarettes.

"Is everyone here?" Rick shouts into the fetid crowd.

No one answers him. I rock queasily from one foot to the other.

"Anybody missing?" he asks again, and again no one answers.

"Okay," he says, adjusting his position in his chair. "Okay," he repeats, "it has come to our attention…" He pauses, scanning the room to ensure that he has made eye contact with every single unfortunate inhabitant of the room, "…that there has been some drug usage as well as some drug dealing happening here, at our very office."

A murmuring starts up in the assembled crowd.

I squeeze the plastic bag in my pocket tightly in my hand.

"Now," he continues, "this is clearly unacceptable. Clearly—" he says pointedly, "—this will not be tolerated."

Heroin-face is sitting in a chair in front of me. I can't see her face, but I can see her fidgeting conspicuously.

I try to ignore her but am overwhelmed with exasperation at her incapacity to remain cool under pressure.

I clench my back teeth together.

"If anyone here has any information about any of this, please come to me," Rick looks into all of our eyes again. Increasing the volume of his voice he tells us: "Anyone found being associated with this problem will be immediately terminated."

Still clenching the plastic bag, I communicate my guiltlessness and non-involvement by pulling my features into what I hope is an angelic and slightly confused expression.

"Now," Rick folds his hands. "We're going to be coming to your desks following this meeting—" again he looks into all our eyes individually "—and we are going to be searching your belongings."

Heroin-face is fidgeting so much now that I pray she is actually having a seizure or some other emergency that could account for her unmistakably guilt-ridden demeanour.

When we are excused from the meeting, some people walk suspiciously quickly to their desks.

I walk to mine slowly, aware that the conspicuous sprinters are going to be searched first.

When I arrive at my desk, I put my hand calmly back in my pocket and roll the plastic bag into a thin cylinder. I pick a pen from my desk, remove its innards, and carefully slide the rolled plastic bag inside. I put the pen back down in front of me and sit patiently.

When it is my turn to be searched, Rick combs through my desk. He asks me to remove my shoes, and opens my bag without asking. He even opens my packet of cigarettes and checks inside.

"Are you involved in this?" he asks me quietly.

"No sir," I reply compliantly as he shuffles through the papers on my desk and picks up the drug-pregnant pen.

"You sure?" he says, still holding the pen.

"I'm positive," I reply.

"Alright." He puts the pen down and moves onto the next desk.

***

"Hello, this is Lark. I am calling on behalf of—"

"OH, LET ME GUESS! Are you calling on behalf of Krippler Incorporated?" The furious man interrupts me, already shrieking, "The perverted institute of repeatedly pestering guilt-less citizens in their homes?"

"We are a market research institute actually," I correct him.

"And what precisely are you researching the market for? For how many God damn calls it takes to coerce a man INto commit-TING manslaughter?"

"Manslaughter is accidental," I counter, then press on quickly, "Today we are conducting a survey on feline diabetes."

"Oh, I could make it look accidental!"

"Do you or any member of your household own a cat?"

***

"Hello my name is Bianca, I am calling on behalf of—"
They hang up.
"Hello my name is Celia. I am calling on behalf of—"
They hang up.
"Hello my name is Desdemona. I am calling on behalf of—"
They hang up.
"Hello my name is Juliet. I am calling on behalf of—"
They hang up.

***

Ivy is massaging the scar on her foot.

"Do you think that Keats was right about scars adding character?" She frowns up at me.

"No," I reply.

***

My fridge's contents: one rotting onion, half a box of baking soda, a flat bottle of ginger ale, and something that might be salsa.

I have watched Keats open, close, and re-open the fridge door multiple times today. I imagine that he is hoping to find enchanted food has materialized, or that he is trying to muster a recipe creative enough to transform those ingredients into something fit for human consumption.

After his eleventh fridge check, he accepts that he cannot eat a rotten onion marinated with baking soda and salsa.

"Let's go get some pizza," he suggests, after reading the label on the salsa jar and throwing it back into the fridge.

***

We walk to the closest pizza place, stopping outside of it to smoke.

Keats has begun telling me about a conspiracy theory he has about Wi-Fi signals.

"If you're in range of a Wi-Fi signal, you can bet your bottom dollar that you're being tracked..."

I look through the glass window of the Pizza restaurant, tuning him out. Inside the restaurant I see Frank eating pizza alone.

I knock on the glass to get Frank's attention.

He turns to look at me and I wave at him, but he quickly looks back down at his food.

I stop waving, confused by this poor reception.

I watch him rapidly pack up his bag and rush to the door on the other side of the restaurant. He drops it twice on his frantic, graceless way to the door.

Keats, who was watching this interaction, laughs.

"That guy sure did not want to see you," he chuckles.

I frown. "I don't know why he acted that way."

***

Keats and I sit down to eat our pizza.

"So who was that guy?" Keats chews with his mouth open.

"That was Frank." I bite my pizza. "He's a guy I work with."

"What's wrong with him?"

"What do you mean?"

"Like what's his problem?"

"I don't know." I shrug.

"That's pretty weird behaviour," Keats bites into a slice. "Hey, do you think maybe he's following you around? Do you think he wrote you that note?"

"What? No. No way." I shake my head.

"People who act suspiciously are up to shit, Jane," Keats explains, "If someone behaves oddly, you can bet it's for a reason."

***

"Hello my name is Helen."

They hang up.

"Hello my name is Frida."

They hang up.

"Hello my name is Marlee."

***

Rick has once again called squeezed all the employees of Krippler Incorporated into the meeting room.

"Everybody here?" he asks the crowd, scanning the room.

"Anybody missing?"

The jaded roomful of miserable call-centre agents collectedly exhale.

"You'll notice a few people are, in fact, missing," he says ostentatiously. "You might have noticed that neither Freddy or Robin are here."

People in the crowd begin crooning to each other.

I have no idea who Freddy or Robin are, so their absence does not alarm me.

"As I am sure you can deduce," Rick projects his assertive voice, "both Freddy and Robin were caught in possession of illegal substances in our very office."

The tired crowd coos in semi-enthusiastic shock.

"Let this be a lesson to you all!" Rick shouts. "We have a zero tolerance policy here at Krippler Incorporated! If you are found trying to pull the same crap as Freddy or Robin, you too will be fired!"

***

In an attempt to address whatever mysterious rift Frank and I are currently experiencing in our friendship, I walk to his desk to say hello to him.

"Hey Frank," I say.

He looks up at me and the colour in his face begins to fade.

"Uh, hi," he replies, looking down at his fidgeting hands.

"Did you see me the other day? I was waving at you and—"

"Uh, hey, uh," he stumbles over his own words, "I'm really busy right now, and uh…"

"You don't want to talk to me?" I tilt my head in an attempt to catch his eyes and possibly decipher what the hell the problem might be.

"Uh," he avoids my eyes, "not right now, no."

I look into his pale, flustered face and say, "Okay" before leaving him alone.

***

"Hello—"
"Don't you dare—"
"This is Jane calling—"
"I swear to God—"
"On behalf of Krippler Incorporated—"
"Stop talking right now—"

"Today—"

"Leave me alone or so help me, you piece of trash!"

"We are conducting a survey—"

"I will make you live to regret this!"

"On feline diabetes."

"REMOVE ME FROM YOUR CALLING LIST."

"Do you—"

"REMOVE ME."

"Or any member of your household—"

"I SWEAR TO GOD JANE."

"Own a cat?"

***

Keats is writhing on the couch, moaning.

Today his paranoia has driven him to believe that Ivy is cheating on him.

"She thinks I'm an idiot," he says, scanning through their text messages.

He then relays a section of their recent conversation that he found particularly suspicious. "She said 'you looked nice today.'"

Unsure of why that remark would upset him, I squint.

"Look at me," he wails, gesturing to the infant-sized coffee stain on the chest of his shirt. "I look like absolute shit today."

I laugh a little. "Maybe she thinks that you look nice regardless."

"I think she meant to send that to someone else." He glares at his phone.

After a moment of silence, wherein I assumed that we had completed our exchange about Ivy's suspected infidelity, Keats whines, "She's sleeping with someone else." He then rolls onto his side, clutching his stomach.

"No she is not." I watch him pathetically pulling fistfuls of his own hair out.

"Don't patronize me, Jane," he says, almost in tears. "Don't pretend like you don't know it too."

I say nothing.

He closes his eyes for a moment, grimacing.

"You and Ivy are both shady!" he shouts abruptly.

I snort. "Pardon me?"

Why have I been dragged into this?

"I don't trust either of you!" He slaps a cup off the table. "I don't trust either of you as far as I can throw you! You're both secretive and manipulative!"

***

"Hello my name is Marcie. I am calling on behalf of—"

They hang up.

"Hello my name is Lucy. I am calling on behalf of—"

They hang up.

"Hello my name is Sally. I am calling on behalf of—"

They hang up.

"Hello my name is Peppermint. I am calling on behalf of—"

"Your name is Peppermint?"

"Yes, hello. I am calling on behalf of Krippler Incorporated. Today we are conducting—"

"Were your parents aware that they were naming you after a fragrant plant?"

I pause. "There are actually quite a number of well-received fragrant plant names, sir. Rose, for example. Daisy."

"What is it that you want, Peppermint?"

"I'm conducting a survey."

"On stripper names?"

"Peppermint is the name of a cartoon child in the Peanuts comics," I explain, "If you, for whatever deviant reason, feel compelled to sexualize that, then that indignity is on you."

"Can I please speak to your manager?"

I hang up.

"Hello my name is Peggy. I am calling on behalf of…"

***

Haley has not yet been caught peddling drugs at work. She is flouncing around the office like a pompous cat, chest puffed out, head held high, and nose to the ceiling. She is clearly proud of her undercover operation's continued success. So unmistakeably proud I am mystified by the managers' ignorance of her guilt.

After work today she said, "I've got you something, if you're into it," and then she sold me five ladybug pills.

In order to ensure that I was not caught with the pills and consequently fired, I made the responsible decision to take all five pills immediately.

***

The bus I am riding on must be on its way to a beauty pageant. Never has a more attractive assemblage of people ever congregated on public transport.

"I wore a blue baby's shirt with a picture of a frog on it," I tell the man sitting next to me.

He grins. "That sounds cute."

"If you, for whatever deviant reason, feel compelled to sexualize that, then that indignity is on you."

He laughs.

"I had a mason jar with a hole in the lid that I sucked through, filled with what I thought was juice."

"Was it alcohol? Are you drunk?" He keeps grinning at me.

"And I wore candy necklaces in my hair like pig tails," I continue, my voice slurring. "I would pull the elastic necklace down from my hair into my mouth and chew off the candies."

"You're cute," he laughs again.

"The woman whose child I babysat washed my knees with alcohol. I used to wear her bras and lipstick and pretend that I was a mother and a wife."

He has his arm around my shoulder.

"I went to the doctor's appointment and was blindsided when he told me that I was pregnant. More blindsided than your typical pregnant thirteen-year-old..."

"Jesus," the guy nudges another male passenger's shoulder.

I assume the other passenger is his friend.

He mouthes, "This girl is fuuucked."

"You know, I have a secret," I tell him, glancing at his friend to make sure he isn't listening.

"Oh yeah? What is it?"

I whisper into his ear, "I am not that small a girl."

***

My bus-friend is holding my arms above my head and spinning me around. The street lights are all circling with me. The stars and the moon are dizzy too.

"Have you been drinking?" he asks me while he bends me backwards over his knee.

"Are you a ballerina?" I request in return, slyly and successfully dodging his question.

I am spinning in the middle of the street on the tips of my toes. My arms are raised above my head and all my fingertips are touching. I spin around and around like a top, held upright by the bus-man.

"Hey, are you a ballerina?" He grins at me.

***

Heroin-face is hovering around my desk like a peckish seagull.

"How did you like those ladybugs, baby?" she asks me quietly, picking up my empty mug and sniffing it.

I have a headache.

"Do you think they have any affect when taken with the morning after pill?" I ask her.

She looks at me blankly for a minute before letting out a loud, short laugh.

"I don't know, baby," she cackles. "Sounds like you did have a good time though, eh?"

I did not have a good time.

"Whose number is this?" She gestures towards the post-it note stuck to my computer.

I cannot muster the energy required to respond.

"Why is this number sticking to your computer?" she repeats. "Is it your boyfriend's number?"

Frank's head slowly peeks over our shared cubical wall.

"That's the number of a guy that I called once to interview," he tells her quietly.

Frank hasn't spoken to me for a few days so I try to catch his eye and smile at him in an effort to mend whatever issue he has with me.

She unsticks the note to examine my artwork more closely. "Why would Jane save the number of a guy who you interviewed?"

Frank looks into my eyes and then quickly looks away.

"'Cause..." he begins, looking pained, "...'cause the guy call me a mongoloid and a retard."

"He called you a retard?" She turns to me. "Why are you keeping the number of a guy who called Frank a retard?"

I am too exhausted to speak to this horrible woman, but I somehow manage to gather the energy required to shrug at her.

"Jane told me to give her his number to teach him a lesson. She's really showing him."

Heroin-face smirks. "Oh really? What are you doing to teach him a lesson?"

Frank replies on my behalf. "She calls him like eleven times a day."

***

"How is everything?" my probation counselor asks perkily.

"Everything's great, thank you."

"No relapses? Any angry thoughts?"

"Nope, none."

"Still eating kale?"

"What?"

"Kale," she says again, "you were raving about kale."

"Ohh," I tilt my head backwards, "Yes, of course. Kale. I still can't get enough of it."

***

"What are you on probation for anyways?" Keats asks me while passing me a large, pink bong.

"Well, do you remember that stock market crisis of 2004?" I reply, positioning the barrel to my mouth.

"My parents were associated with what's called the "Y component", which—as I am sure you know—played a major role in the downsizing of a number of really prominent fortune 500 companies. I doubt I need to name them. I took responsibility for something I shouldn't have and managed to land myself in a small detention centre. I got out a little early for good behaviour, thankfully. I was just a kid, right? They're a little more lenient when you haven't reached whatever age it is when your frontal lobes are fully developed."

"Ah," he says, narrowing his eyes, "that's a bummer."

***

"What are you on probation for again?" Ivy asks me over the phone.

"Possession of coke," I reply quickly. "It wasn't even mine, but I guess everyone says that, right? I was going to a party with a small group of girls. The girls were all a little older than me. I'd met them at a summer camp the year before. Anyways, I brought a purse to the party. None of the other girls did. So, of course, I ended up carrying all their stuff—which, unfortunately for me, included coke. That little favour landed me in a detention centre for a significant portion of my adolescence. But what can you do, eh?"

"That's rough," she replies.

***

"Hello my name is Marge. I am calling on behalf of—"
They hang up.
"Hello my name is Lisa. I am calling on behalf of Krippler Incorporated. Today—"
They hang up.
"Hello my name is Maude."
They hang up.

***

"Where the hell are all the knives, Jane?" Keats storms into my bedroom.

I have piled Cheetos on the front of my shirt and am eating them lying down.

"Where the fuck are they?" he asks me again.

"What's troubling you, Keats?" I look at him, my cheeks stuffed like a hamster's.

He stares at me. "Have you taken all of the knives?"

I pause, mid-chew, then scowl. "No, I haven't taken all of the knives."

"Then where the hell are they?"

"I suspect that they're at the base of the mountain of molding dishes that you've been growing in the sink."

Keats never washes the dishes. I once stopped washing them just to see how long he would go without doing them. It was a shocking two and a half months before I caved in and did them myself.

He stares at me.

"Are you cutting yourself again?" he asks me.

Exasperation surges through my entire body.

"Are you?" he asks me, louder this time.

I stand up. Cheetos fall to my feet like cheesy confetti.

"Are you!"

I point both middle fingers up and spin to the washroom.

***

I have taken the knives.

***

"Hello my name is Alma. I am calling on behalf of—" I begin.

"—You have reached Benjamin. If you are calling from Krippler Incorporated or any of its affiliates, I demand that you remove me from your calling list! For personal and business inquiries, please leave your name, number, and the reason for your call."

I wait for the beep.

"Hello Benjamin. This is Jane calling on behalf of Krippler Incorporated. We will call you back at a better time to discuss a study we are conducting on feline diabetes. Take care."

***

My phone rings.

"Hello?"

No-one responds.

"Hello?" I repeat.

Again, nobody answers.

"Ivy?"
No answer.
"Frank?" I ask quietly.
Nothing.

***

"Hello my name is Elizabeth. I am calling on behalf of Krippler Incorporated, a market research institute. Today we are conducting a survey on feline diabetes. Do you, or any member of your household, own a cat?"
A man laughs. "Yeah, sure, hold on a sec."
He then puts the receiver down and I sit listening to the background noises of his home for two hours and fifteen minutes.

***

I am moving my legs in the bathtub, making waves. A tidal wave of bathwater. A hurricane. Today's shape to adorn my thighs with is: the flower.
Hello, this is Petunia calling on behalf of the garden. Today we are conducting a survey on ladybugs. Are you, or any members of your household, high?

***

"Hello my name is Hermione. I am calling on behalf of Krippler Incorporated, a market research institute. Today we are conducting a survey on feline diabetes. Do you, or any member of your household, own a cat?"
"All of the cat owners are dead," replies a boy whose voice is indicative of his current bout with puberty.
"Please accept my apology—" I begin to say while he hangs up on me.

***

"Hello?" I answer my phone.
"Hi Jane," replies a quiet voice.
"Who is this?" I ask.
They don't reply.
"Who is this?" I ask again.
Nothing.

***

Ivy and Keats are hosting an Ugly Christmas Sweater party. My apartment is currently overrun with shoddily dressed strangers. The only infestation more trying than rats is an infestation of people wearing sweaters that light up and play "Jingle Bells".

One guest is sporting a sweater that is not ugly at all. She saw her opportunity to look better than all her friends and she took it. She stands out against the homely crowd like the star of Bethlehem.

"That's a beautiful sweater," I say to her under my breath when she passes me.

I am standing at the kitchen table, adjacent to a group of people and, more importantly, a tray of shortbread cookies.

While I gnaw the limbs off of pastry angel, Ivy asks me, "Hey, how was your probation meeting?"

Everyone looks round at me.

Bothered not only by the public airing of my personal affairs, but also by the harsh realization that these are actually sugar cookies, I scowl.

"It was fine, Ivy. How was your recent abortion?"

She snorts boisterously. "Oh my God, you're hilarious, Jane."

I spend the rest of the evening discussing my police record with total strangers.

"What are you on probation for?"
"I got caught with weed once."

"What are you on probation for?"
"Shoplifting."
"What are you on probation for?"
"Drunk driving."
"What are you on probation for?"
"Underage drinking."
"What are you on probation for?"
"I brought a gun to school."
"What are you on probation for?"
"Killing everyone at a Christmas party."

***

Ivy invited Brian to the party. I have noticed him staring at me when he thinks I'm not looking. Every time I see him approaching me I move rooms.

***

After I have devoted an adequate amount of time attempting to converse with the unwelcome herd, I leave the party to find refuge in my bedroom. Upon entering my would-be safe haven, however, I discover that it has been infiltrated.

There are three girls sitting on my bed and snorting coke off one of my books.

"Hey! Knock!" a girl with a pierced nose shouts at me.

"This is my room." I lock eyes with her.

Her nose is pierced with a loop in the columella, in a sort of bovine fashion.

She laughs girlishly. "Oh, I'm so sorry. I didn't realize. Do want some snow?"

"Snow?"

"Yeah, girl. We're just trying to stick with the holiday theme," she giggles, "got a problem?"

She then hands me my own collection of fairy tales, which they have been using as a sort of platter. White dust forms a thick line down the middle of Cinderella's cheerful, grinning face.

I position a rolled fifty-dollar bill in my nostril.

Someone knocks on the door. We ignore it. The person knocks again and then enters uninvited.

It's Brian.

He looks at me wiping my nose and frowns. "Don't get into that, Jane."

"Into what?"

"You don't need to do this shit, do you?"

I shrug. "I don't need to do anything."

"Why don't you come hang out with me then?"

"I'm too busy."

"Is this your room?" He begins looking around.

One of the girls interrupts Brian, saying, "Coke makes me feel so gay! Do any of you girls feel that way?"

I laugh really loudly. "Maybe you're just actually gay?"

Brian squeezes in next to me. "So do you read a lot?" he asks, nodding towards the books beside my bed.

I ignore him and turn to the girl who said she felt gay and kiss her. I pin her arms above her head and climb on top of her.

She starts biting my lower lip.

"That hurts a little," I tell her after she has successfully chewed my lower lip to a steady bleed.

She is either insensitive or didn't hear me.

Hi ho sailor.

Sail me away.

***

Hours have passed. I am now sitting on the couch in the living room and Brian is standing at the apartment door, preparing to leave.

"Bye Jane," he says before walking through the door.

***

"Hello my name is Myra."
They hang up.
"Hello my name is Karla."
They hang up.
"Hello my name is Beverly."
They hang up.
"Hello my name is Caverly."
They hang up.

***

"Hello, my name is Delilah, I am calling on behalf of—"
"It's Christmas Eve, scumbag!"
"Hello, my name is Hagar—"
"It's Christmas Eve, dick!"
"Hello, my name is Jezebel—"
"It's Christmas Eve, deadbeat!"
"Hello, my name is Ruth—"
"It's Christmas Eve, prick!"
"Hello, my name is Mary—"
"It's Christmas Eve, motherfucker!"

***

Ivy and Keats are having gratuitously loud sex. The paper-thin
wall is proving ineffective as a sound barrier. I wonder if, in fact,
it is somehow amplifying the sound.
Keats keeps moaning, "I love you."
Ivy keeps moaning, "Fuck me."
I keep moaning, "Jesus Christ."

***

There are ladybugs crawling all over my bed. My hair has ladybugs in it. I can feel ladybugs crawling between my toes. They are making ladybug homes in my shoes. I can hear them talking about ladybug politics.

Keats keeps moaning, "I love you."

Ivy keeps moaning, "Fuck me."

I keep moaning, "Jesus Christ."

***

I wake up with a pounding head and wander into the living room.

Ivy and Keats are sitting on the couch. Both are holding gifts.

"Oh, sorry," I murmur, turning to leave.

"No, no, stay!" Ivy insists.

"No," I reply.

"Stay!" Keats demands.

"Fine," I reply, feeling too queasy to argue further.

Keats unwraps his present from Ivy first. To my intense distaste, it is black lingerie. Presumably Ivy will be the one wearing it, but who knows? Not me, and I don't want to either. I look away.

"No really, I'd prefer to leave." I begin to stand up.

Ivy shushes me. "Don't be a prude."

Smiling feverishly, she announces, "My turn!" and begins opening her gift from Keats.

The room is silent as a Tweety bird patterned steering wheel cover is unveiled.

Ivy has never expressed any interest in Looney Tunes, or, as far as I know, birds in general.

"Tweety bird?" she says breathlessly, after a pause long enough to declare a person who has stopped breathing dead.

"He's cute, eh?" Keats smiles at her, bathing in the glow of his own generosity.

"Yeah." Ivy swallows loudly. "Tweety's cute. Sure. "

Despite the fact that that Keats' gift to Ivy was probably pillaged from a dumpster, Ivy forces a smile and says, "You know, I used to watch Looney Tunes with my mom every Sunday morning."

Ivy's sad attempt at optimism after being given the worst gift ever wrapped makes me smile a little, despite it all.

"Oh yeah? Me too," I lie.

"Really?" She grins at me. "That's a nice memory to have of your mom, eh?"

I nod.

"Tell me more about your mom," she probes, putting her new piece of garbage carefully down.

"Alright." I nod. "Alright, well, my parents were both political activists—I've probably mentioned? They made some serious sacrifices for the rights of Canadians—"

"Is that true?" Keats interrupts me.

"Yes." I stretch my arms in a yawn. "But you take a serious risk when you get involved in that kind of thing. To this day I still believe their politics influenced why they died—"

"I thought they died of a disease?" Keats interrupts me again.

I nod. "Yeah, well when you work as much as they did it has an impact on your immune system."

***

My phone is ringing.

"Hello?"

"Hi Jane."

"Who is this?"

"Hi Jane."

"Hi. Who's calling?"

"Hello Jane."

I hang up.

***

Keats, Ivy, and I are lying on the living room floor drinking eggnog from coffee mugs. My mug has two ladybug pills dissolved in it.

"What did your family do for Christmas when you were a kid?" Ivy asks me. "Did your dad dress up like Santa or anything?"

I shake my head. "No."

"My family always makes a float for the city's parade," she says. "A carwash float. Can you believe that? It's so embarrassing. They make me ride on it."

"My family carols," Keats interjects. "They fucking carol."

Ivy rolls onto her stomach. "What was your favourite Christmas present that you ever got? Mine was my easy-bake oven. Easily."

Keats replies quickly, "A red, child-sized convertible."

I say nothing.

"What about you, Jane?" Ivy asks.

"I don't remember." I sip from my mug.

We put more rum in our drinks than eggnog and my face feels hot.

"Come on." Keats nods at me. "Open up a little. It's Christmas. What was your favourite present?"

"I never got presents," I admit.

"Why not?" Ivy frowns.

I shrug.

***

"Hello, my name is Darlene. I am calling on behalf of—"

"Is this Jane?"

"Yes, hello."

"Listen," the man growls under his breath, "I want you to use your ears, Jane. Your ears are those two pieces of flesh attached to the sides of your presumably very thick head, okay Jane? I want my number removed from your satanic calling list. Okay? I want to be removed for good. Do you hear me right now?"

"We don't have a calling list, sir."

"No, now you're not listening to me, Jane. I said: Remove. Me. From. Your. Calling. List."

"We don't have a calling list."

"REMOVE ME FROM YOUR CALLING LIST."

"Sir," I say coolly.

"What?" he says, now panting.

"We don't have a calling list."

"I AM GOING TO FIND OUT WHERE YOU LIVE, JANE! MARK MY WORDS. I AM GOING TO BOTHER YOU IN YOUR OWN GODDAMN GODFORSAKEN HOME. YOU WILL REGRET EVER CALLING ME. YOU CAN MARK MY WORDS!"

He slams his phone down.

***

"Hello, this is Jane calling—"

"STOP IT."

***

"Look who I brought over!" Ivy announces jauntily as she enters the apartment with Brian.

Brian waves.

Keats acknowledges Brian's presence by forming gun shapes with his hands and shooting at him.

I acknowledge his presence by frowning.

Why Ivy feels this compulsion to force Brian and me together bewilders me. I think Ivy imagines that all girls are desperate to be paired off. I can't imagine wanting anything more than I want to be alone.

"How are you, Jane?" Brian asks.

"I'm good," I say without looking at him. "How are you?"

"I'm good too, thank you." He sits down on the couch beside me.

His weight pulls me towards the centre of the couch. I have to struggle uncomfortably to remain on my designated cushion.

***

I leave the living room to go to the washroom. Immediately after I have shut the door, Ivy knocks. She then shuffles inside with a small plastic bag and a grin.

***

"Would you like to go the movies with me sometime?" Brian asks me.

Keats and Ivy are dancing in the kitchen while cooking spaghetti.

My head feels like it is too heavy for my neck. I lean it back to rest on a cushion.

"We could go out for dinner, if you want," he continues. "Do you like Mexican food?"

I laugh.

"Can I get you some water?"

I laugh again.

I feel like my skin is heavy.

A glass of water has appeared in my hand.

"Are you okay?" he asks me.

I keep seeing lightning.

"Is there a storm?" I ask.

Brian shakes his head.

"I think you need to go to bed," he tells me.

He walks me down the hallway to my room. Our arms are linked.

"Where are you going?" I ask him after lying down in my bed.

He pulls my blanket over me and begins walking towards the door.

"Where are you going?" I ask him again.

He turns off my light and shuts the door softly behind him.

***

Ivy's taken me to her parent's house. I asked to wait in her car for her, but she insisted that I come inside.

I was originally lured into her car with the promise of a burrito. Ivy did not mention going to her parent's house at all. She had only said, "Hop in Jane, we're getting burritos." Blinded by my affection for burritos, I jumped into the car like an unwitting pig on its way to a slaughterhouse.

The back of my hair is matted. I have mis-buttoned my flannel shirt, so it is clutching gawkily at parts of my torso and hanging loosely from others. There are gaps between buttons revealing segments of bare skin. I stand out against this wholesome family backdrop like a dishevelled homeless woman.

Ivy is in the next room, packing an "overnight bag" to bring back to our apartment. I got a glimpse of the bag that she's using and I noted that it would also be convenient as luggage for a person taking a transatlantic flight, or a murderer transporting a body.

I am standing in the living room, staring at a brown and decomposing Christmas tree, and trying to ease my growing concern that one of Ivy's family is going to come home early, see me, and assume based on my appearance that I am here to rob them. I am mentally reciting what I will say if this transpires.

"Hello. Please stay calm. I'm Ivy's friend. I only look like this because I have just been robbed."

Apart from the dead tree, Ivy's house is a beautiful suburban family home. It exists in the same universe as commercials for gourmet cat food. Wooden floors and white walls and real sunflowers in glass vases. The faint, lingering smell of decades of home-baked cookies has bled into the clean, tall walls.

The house is overrun with hundreds of family photos. Child-Ivy grins at me from all angles. In one photo she has pudding smudged all over her healthy, baby cheeks. She and her happy sisters smile at me from the beach. They are wearing neon one-piece bathing suits, standing proudly next to the small, crumbling sandcastles they have made.

There is also whole row of professional family photos staring at me. Each picture shows everyone in this idyllic family growing and aging year by year. There are hundreds of snapshots of smiling, happy little girls and happy, proud parents. They are watching me looking at them, smiling away.

I amble around the house, following the photos, until I reach a white bathroom. I go inside and shut the door.

Behind the bathroom mirror I find expired Ambien and fresh Prozac. In front of it, I find that no-one who has crossed paths with me today has had the decorum to mention that I have a very conspicuous blue pen mark drawn across my cheek.

***

"Did you steal some pills from Ivy's house today?" Keats confronts me in the living room.

"What?" I look up from my book.

"Did you steal some pills from Ivy's house?" he asks me again, now crossing his arms.

"Did Ivy say that I did?"

"She said she wondered if you had. She's too afraid to accuse you in case it offends you."

"It does offend me." I look back down at my book.

"Be honest. Did you do it?"

"Of course I didn't, Keats. Who do you think I am?"

***

"Hello my name is Bonnie Parker."
They hang up.
"Hello my name is Ma Barker."

They hang up.

***

"Hello, my name is Jane. I am calling on behalf of Krippler Incorporated, a market research institute—"

"No," the man sneers. "No!" louder this time, "I am waiting for an essential phone call, Jane! If you continue to mercilessly phone me, my line will be busy and I will miss the call! Are you capable of comprehending words, Jane? ARE YOU PROCESSING WHAT I AM SAYING RIGHT NOW?"

"Today we're conducting a survey—"

"NO!" he screams as he hangs up.

***

"Hello, my name is Jane. I'm—"

"You insolent whore!" the man screams as he slams his phone down.

***

"Hello, my name is Jane."
He hangs up.

***

"Hello, my name is Jane."
"Stop it!"

***

"Hello."
"YOU ARE GOING TO REGRET THIS, JANE."

I arrive home to once again witness Keats casually ambling out of my bedroom.

He stops in his tracks when our eyes connect.

"I was just looking for a lighter!" he shrieks defensively. "Goddammit, Jane, can't I even look for a lighter?"

I grit my back molars. "Go buy yourself a lighter if you can't find one, Keats. Rub some sticks together."

"Did you take those pills from Ivy?" he asks me loudly, puffing out his chest. "Admit it if you did it! Did you steal from Ivy's house?"

"No."

"Why are you being so weird about your room then? What are you hiding in there, if not those pills!"

"Stay out of my room, Keats."

"Why are you so private? What are you hiding! What's your big secret? Are you keeping bodies in there? Do you have some sort of undercover drug operation going on? Are you a cop, Jane? Is that it?"

I clench my jaw.

His chest is moving up and down rapidly. The combination of illogical panic and excessive yelling is making him hyperventilate.

He inhales loudly and croakily, looks me dead in the eye, and asks me, "Is Jane your real name?"

***

"Hello, my name is Nancy Drew."
They hang up.
"Hello, my name is Modesty Blaise."
They hang up.

***

"I know you didn't take anything from my parent's medicine cabinet," Ivy tells me over the phone while I chew on the pills that I stole. "I want to apologize for Keats. He shouldn't have accused you of that."

I say nothing.

"Do you want to come to a party with me tonight? I'll share my wine with you, to make up for this."

I shrug to myself. "Okay, what kind of party is it?"

"It's at a farm."

"A farm?"

"It'll be fun," she defends the farm., "we'll run around in the field like snow pixies."

***

Dancing in the snow fields, I am now a pixie.

Spinning and sipping from the spout of Ivy's wine bottle, I spin, sip, spin.   Brian is, unfortunately, a pixie in the snowfields too.

"You look really nice today," he tells me.

***

The music that is playing is slow and the lyrics are sad.

Brian gave me some of his Canadian Club to drink. He is sitting beside me. Ivy is still dancing in the snow.

The party is big. There are a number of fire pits dotted across the fields. Brian and I are sitting in front of one of them.

"I used to make fires with my sisters when I was a kid," he shares with me, "I have a very strong, positive association with fire. My sisters and I would make little campfires in the woods. We'd cook marshmallows together."

I am barely listening. The hum of his babbling voice ebbs into my lethargic mind. The words warp into whale sounds.

I watch the fire crack and I sip my drink.

Periodically, Brian turns and speaks to me like an attentive husband:

"Are you having a nice night, Jane?"

"Can I get you anything?"

"You look really nice tonight."

"I'm having a great time talking with you."

I suspect that Ivy has lied to him and misled him into thinking that I have expressed an interest in him. His persistence and unfounded interest in me suggests that I have become a pawn in some sort of Cosmo-magazine inspired matchmaking experiment.

I wonder why he likes me. Maybe he has misdiagnosed my quiet demeanour, assuming that my silence is a symptom of a shy and gentle soul. In reality, my quietness is a consequence of my deeply entrenched nihilism. I don't believe there is any real value in my or anyone else's speaking, and I think that all of human existence is fundamentally unimportant. I consider telling him this to see if it shuts him up.

"Can I get you another drink?" he asks me politely.

I look at his face. His teeth are straight and white.

He smiles at me. "Can I get you another drink, Jane?" he asks me again.

"Yeah, sure."

***

There are Christmas lights strung in the haystack.

Brian took me up here to show me the view from a window. We can see all of the fire pits and everyone dancing.

"See?" he says, gesturing out the window, smiling. "It's pretty, isn't it?"

I nod.

"Do you want to go find Ivy?" he asks me, checking that I am happy in his company, and that I do not need an excuse to escape him.

"No," I reply.

"Are you sure?"

***

"Are you okay with this?" he asks me.

"Yeah."

He puts his hand between my legs and leans me backwards.

I look up through the window.

"Are you sure you're okay?" He stops and asks me again.

I look down at him. "Yeah." I say again.

"You're comfortable?"

I squint at him. "Yes."

"I don't want you to feel pressured," he continues.

"I'm fine, Brian. Thank you."

"Sorry, I just want to make sure."

I squint at his face and tilt my head. "Why do you like me?" I ask him.

He smiles. "Because."

***

I feel abnormally aware of the air in my lungs and of the blood in my body. Brian's breath is loud and reminds me that he is a person and that he is alive and so am I.

I put his hand on my throat to stop my breath and try to subdue this feeling of being a person who breathes and takes up space and fucks people, but he won't keep his hand there. He moves it to my waist and kisses my forehead.

I feel a cold rush down my body and suddenly I'm panicked. I wonder if Brian has ever been with a girl who loved him before. I wonder if there is a person out in the world who would feel sick at the thought of him being naked with me. I cannot shake this thought. I become sure of it. I suddenly feel a sickening, overwhelming guilt. I have to close my eyes to stop from crying at the thought of the girl I have imagined.

"Is my mouth stained?" my voice cracks.

"What?" He stops.

"Is there colour on my mouth?" I ask, rubbing roughly at my lip.

"No, there's nothing there." He looks at me.

"I feel like there's pink lipstick all over my fingers." I look down at my hands, in tears now.

***

"Don't invite me to places Brian is anymore," I tell Ivy.

***

Ladybugs bleed from their knees when they're threatened.
My teeth taste like rusty metal and uncoated Tylenol.

***

I am spinning in the middle of the street on the tips of my toes. My arms are raised above my head and all of my fingertips are touching. I spin around and around like a top.

"Hey, are you a ballerina?" The man grins at me while shoving me onto the curb. I land gracelessly on the concrete. The road scrapes a sort of rug burn into the back of my thighs.

His entire weight is pressed down on top of me, crushing my ribs and my hips.

"Get off," I breathe quietly.

"You've got cuts all over you," he points out while tugging at my clothes. "Do you do this to yourself?"

"I do, yeah." I nod. "The first time I cut my legs it was with my father's switch blade."

"That's weird." He shoves his face into my collarbone while unzipping his pants.

I laugh to myself. "I did it so I could knock on the Arwol's door and tell Mrs. Arwol that I was hurt."

"What?"

"When I was little I accidently cut my knees so I knocked on the Arwol's door to ask for help. Mrs. Arwol put alcohol and Band-Aids on my knees. I cut myself on purpose with my dad's switch blade so she'd take care of me again."

He's ignoring me.

"Mr. Arwol answered the door this time though, and he took me inside."

I continue telling him my story while he writhes around on top of me, not paying any attention to what I am trying to tell him.

"My mother kept warm vodka in her closet and I'd drink it and throw up in the bathroom sink," I explain. I imitate my mother's shrill voice: 'Why do you keep fucking puking in the sink?' she was always saying to me. 'Every fucking day you're puking in the sink'."

He puts his hand on my throat.

I choke. "I told Mr. Arwol that the first bra I owned was one that I stole from his wife."

I laugh while struggling to breathe: "I told Mr. Arwol, 'Did you know that you smell like laundry detergent and banana medicine? You smell like someone who is being cared for.'"

I close my eyes and cackle to myself about my damaged childhood. "I cut myself so Mrs. Arwol would kiss my knees!"

He tightens his grip on my throat.

I croak. "I told Mr. Arwol 'I don't really need any help but maybe you could show me how it feels to be a mother and a wife.'"

***

"What are you on probation for again?" Keats asks me.
"I've already told you that," I reply.
"Right," he glares at me, "right, sure you did."

***

"Did you graduate from high school?" Keats asks me.
"Yes, I did. Why do you ask?"
"I just wondered," he says. "I just wondered, that's all."

***

"What's your middle name again?" Keats asks me.
"It is mind your own business."
"Right," Keats replies. "Sure."

***

My phone is ringing.
"Yes?" I say into it.
Nothing.
"Hello?"

***

"Hello?" My phone again.
"Hi Jane," a voice answers this time.
"Who is this?" I ask.
I can hear breathing.
"Who is this?"
No response.
"Hello?"
Nothing.

***

Today heroin-face said, "I got you something, if you're into it."
"What?"

***

I am calling God.
"Hello, this is Jane."
"Hey Jane."
"I'm calling on behalf of—"
"I know why you're calling."
"Right, of course, you're omniscient."
"Will you please stop calling me?"
"I'm doing a survey—"
"I know what you're doing, but I've asked that these calls cease."
"It's on feline diabetes."
"Yes, I know what it's about."
"Do you or any member of your household own a cat?"
"Is that why you're calling?"
"Yes. What are your cats ages?"
"I don't have any cats."
"Oh, please accept my apology."
"I can't talk to you right now, Jane."
"Okay, please accept my apology."
"Stop calling me all the time, okay Jane?"
"Okay, please accept my apology."
"Please accept my apology."
The line goes dead.
"Please accept my apology."

***

I arrive at the office unprepared for another hellish shift. As I pass through the foyer, I notice Frank sitting sombrely by the receptionist's desk. His face is flushed and there are drying tear tracks drawn down his purple cheeks. His legs are sprawled out straight, and his arms are lying limp and defeated at his sides.

"What's going on Frank?" I ask him.

He pretends not to hear me and stares vacantly ahead.

"Are you okay?" I ask.

He continues to ignore me, but blinks. The closing of his eyelids force some silent tears to travel down his purple cheeks and fall off the edge of his jaw.

***

Unable to spend my entire shift struggling to console Frank, I have taken my seat at my desk.

Witnessing a disabled man cry has disheartened me. In an effort to lift my own spirits, I begin to dial the number attached to my screen.

"Hello, this is Jane calling on behalf of—"

Suddenly the office is overtaken by a sharp wailing sound, similar to the noise a dog might make if it were hit by a car.

"What the hell is going on there?" The respondent shouts into my ear, presumably in response to the violent background noise.

"I don't know," I answer him, "Hold on a sec."

"I WILL NOT HOLD—"

I press the hold button.

I stand up and scan the sea of cubicles, searching for the source of the noise. Other employees are also peering over their own cubicle walls. We exchange concerned expressions.

Frank is being walked down an aisle in the middle of the office by two large male managers. He is hysterical. His face is contorted and red. A heavy stream of tears flows down his sweating, distressed face.

"Well Frank's been fired!" One of the managers shouts over Frank's distraught cries. "Some sicko in here sold coke to a mentally disabled guy, and now he's out of work!"

Frank's eyes are tightly squinted and his bottom lip protruded. He is having trouble holding himself up. The managers are holding an arm each and taking his weight.

"Hope you feel good about yourself!" One of the managers shouts throughout the room, while struggling to prop Frank up. "Hope you feel real good about what you've done to this poor, dumb man!"

"He's out of work!" the other manager chimes in. "No one's going to hire a mentally challenged coke addict! Whoever did this should be ashamed of themselves!"

Frank's shrill cries echo through the room.

People begin to shout at the managers.

"Give him a break!"

"Jesus Christ, he probably doesn't even know what he bought!"

The office is in an uproar. No-one is on the phone.

"Don't fire Frank!"

These protests are ignored and the managers continue dragging Frank towards the exit.

When Frank and they are passing by my desk, Frank finally looks at me. His eyes are bloodshot and his bottom lip is quivering.

"I am so sorry" he chokes, looking at me. He is having difficulty breathing.

"Do you even know what coke is, Frank?" I ask him.

The managers are busy propping him up and shouting at the office to settle down.

"Go back to your calls!" one of them screams. "Everyone, get back to work!"

Frank shakes his head. "I dunno!"

"Why did you buy it then?" I ask quietly. "Why'd you buy that?"

"I didn't buy anything! That's the problem!" he sobs, "I'm getting fired for stealing pens again" he cries, inhaling irregularly.

"What? No you're not," I say.

He shakes his wet, red head frenziedly. "I'm so sorry I stole your pen."

"What?" I squint at him, confused.

"I keep getting fired for stealing pens!" he wails hysterically.

My stomach jolts as I remember the pen I hid coke in.

"What do you mean you stole my pen?" I ask quietly.

He's too beside himself to speak clearly. "I took your pen!" he cries. "I am so sorry. I just can't help myself! I saw a nice pen on your desk and I took it! I can't believe I'm getting fired for stealing pens again!"

The managers with him are both too busy trying to tame the room to hear Frank's interaction with me.

Unable to think of anything to say, I watch as they drag him out of the office. His muffled howls continue to ring through the office as he is removed from the property.

***

I hear a small, abrupt bang on my bedroom door.

"Hello?" I sit up.

I hear it again.

"Hello?" I shout again.

Keats opens my door slowly.

"Alright Jane," he says, "just tell me. Just tell me if you're working for the government."

"What?"

He stares at me without blinking. "I've been looking into your past." He nods, eyes wide. "That's right. And it's shady, Jane. Boy, is it shady."

I squint at him.

"You lie about everything!" he shouts. "You can't keep any of your ridiculous stories straight!"

I squint at him.

"Do you work for the government?" he asks me again sternly. "Tell me if you do. Just say it!"

"Yeah," I nod, "yeah, I'm with the FBI. I'm here about your grand plans to undermine our genetically modified tomato scheme. The government is extremely interested in you."

"Is Jane your real name?"

I sigh.

"Is it?"

I squint at him again.

"I looked up your school alumni records," he explains. "You aren't listed. Pre-school. Elementary. High school. You don't exist. No birth certificate."

I squint some more.

He leans forward. "Explain it, Jane. Explain why you don't exist."

"I didn't graduate school," I admit.

"You aren't listed as ever being a student. As ever being a student, in any school, in all of Canada!"

"Names slip by, Keats," I explain. "Elementary schools' records might not be up to your high standards."

He leans in closer to me. "They appear to keep immaculate records. Is Jane short for something?"

I squint at him.

"You are hiding something..." His eyes widen. "Tell me your real name!"

I ignore him.

"What's your real name?" he demands again.

"It's Samantha," I answer truthfully. "I had it changed."

He stares blankly at me for a full minute, mouth ajar, astounded that one of his suspicions has finally proven accurate.

"Why?" he asks breathlessly, "Why did you have it changed?"

"I wanted a new name after I got out of prison."

"Why? What were you trying to hide?"

I laugh. "I was trying to hide my criminal history, obviously, Keats. I didn't want to keep the same name I had when I was put in prison."

"Who changes their name for a juvenile shoplifting charge?"

I exhale out my nose. "It wasn't for shoplifting, you idiot."

"What was it for then? What did you do?"

"I operated a large-scale drug cartel through Eastern Canada—
"

"Be honest!"

"I was involved in insider trade—"

"You're a fucking liar, Jane!" he screams. "Or should I say Samantha."

I punch him in the face.

***

After rummaging around the house, stuffing his belongings into a knapsack, and murmuring statements like, "You are psychotic," Keats has left the apartment to stay indefinitely with his parents.

Before leaving the apartment, he shouted at me in an unsteady, insecure voice: "I want you to move out! I want you gone!"

I have been drinking in the living room since his departure to rejoice in the happiness of my consecrated life.

After finishing my fifth beer my phone rings.

"Hello."

"Hey Jane. It's Ivy."

"Keats isn't home."

"I know, can I come over?"

"Keats and I have had a falling out," I tell her.

"I know, can I come over?"

"If you want to."

I have finished my seventh beer by the time she arrives at the door.

She has brought more alcohol, Kool-Aid, and a bag of assorted pills.

"Where did you get those?" I nod at the pills.

"My grandmother's medicine drawer," she grins.

I also grin.

***

Her teeth and lips are tinted purple from the Kool-Aid. Mine are probably purple too, but I can't see them. You can't see your own face from within it. This is something I have always struggled with.

I have been chewing the pills. Crushing them in my teeth like candies. The dust is compacting inside my molars and in the cracks of my teeth. My mouth tastes sweet from the Kool-Aid, but every so often chunks of pill-dust loosen, fall onto my tongue, and shoot bitterness through the purple tang.

"I like the benzos," I say, looking at the trail mix of medicine that we are snacking on. Benzos are the chocolate chip of the chem-trail mix.

"What else is in there?" I ask.

"Everything," she answers. "Muscle relaxants, Flintstone vitamins, sedatives, Viagra, Ritalin."

We chew the pills and sip the Kool-Aid and lie on the floor.

"I really care about you, you know," she tells me.

I can see motion.

***

BANG.

A thunderous knock on my front door startles me awake.

BANG.

I climb out of my bed and fumble towards the sound, alarmed and dishevelled.

What's behind door number one, ladies and gentlemen?

It is my probation counselor!

And I am still high!

She frowns at me and says, "Oh Jane."

I push my hair out of my face.

***

I have a court date.

***

I have leftover pills!

***

I can see motion!

***

I cut my arms from my elbow to my wrist. Blood is erupting at a pace that I am unfamiliar with.

I just like the feeling. Not to worry, ladies and gentlemen, I am in it merely for the sensation.

I chew four benzos. One. Two. Three. Four.

I chew four more benzos. Five. Six. Seven. Eight.

I could amputate my arm if I were so compelled.

I chew four more benzos. Nine. Ten. Eleven Twelve.

I am the sole owner of all of my own appendages.

I chew ten Tylenol. Thirteen. Fourteen. Fifteen. Sixteen. Seventeen. Eighteen. Nineteen. Twenty. Twenty-One. Twenty-Two.

This is a thing of art, ladies and gentlemen. This is something we should look at with tilted heads and reverent sighs. The sharp colour contrasts against my dull skin in a piercing allusion to everything.

I chew three sedatives. Twenty-three. Twenty-four. Twenty-five.

I chew two no-names. Twenty-six. Twenty-seven.

I chew two sleeping pills. Twenty-eight. Twenty-nine.

The elevator whines while it drops me. It screams in its elevator tongue that it is in desperate need of repairs.

"I am in desperate need of repairs!" we shriek together in a stunning duet, thrilling our audience. Breaking cables are snapping and screaming behind us in a violent choir.

I am plummeting rapidly to the bottom of the elevator shaft. Sparks are flying and the prospect of dying inside of this moving metal coffin is sitting quite well with me. Imminent death in general actually sits quite well with me.

This is how I wanted to go.

***

I open my eyes.

There's a T.V. mounted on the wall beside me. I can smell antiseptic and apple juice.

I am in a hospital.

I sit up and immediately tear the I.V. from my wrist.

A nurse rushes in and touches me.

I throw her hand off me.

"Listen," I start to explain, "I have to leave. I hate hospitals."

She is talking to someone on her nurse's walkie-talkie.

She looks at me pityingly and shakes her head. "No, you can't leave. Sorry."

***

"Please let me leave," I say to a nurse while she meddles with the machinery surrounding me.

"No. Sorry. You can't go yet."

"Please."

"Sorry."

"Please."

***

"I can't sleep here," I explain to the nurse when she brings me water.

"I'm sorry sweetie."

"I need a sleeping pill."

"Sorry sweetie."

***

I sit up in the bed all night.

***

I had to sleep over in the hospital when I was thirteen. I had never slept over in a hospital before.

My bed had railings surrounding it like a crib for pre-teens. I had to wear a paper dress. It was hot and I wasn't allowed to open the window. I said that I felt hot so they gave me apple juice with a tin-foil lid.

I asked my mom if she would stay the night with me but she said no.

I stabbed the tin-foil lid with the end of my straw.

"Please stay the night."

"No."

"Please."

"No."

***

I sat upright in the hospital bed the whole night.

The girl sharing the room with me would not stop crying.

"Are you okay?" I asked her.

She didn't reply.

"Hey, are you okay?"

Nothing.

A nurse checked on her a lot. Every time the nurse came in the room to check on her she would look over at me, but she didn't talk to me until her fourth visit.

"And how about you, honey? Are you feeling okay?"

I shrugged.

She sat down on the bed beside me and patted the top of my leg through the blanket.

I told her I was pregnant and the baby died.

She said, "Oh honey."

I said my mom wouldn't stay the night.

She said, "Oh honey."

I said that I hadn't wanted to be pregnant to begin with, but that I felt sad now.

She said, "Oh honey."

***

In the morning the nurse came back to check on me.

"Are you using contraceptives now?" she asked.

I didn't know what that meant.

She looked at me. "Are you on the birth control pill, honey?"

I shook my head.

She gave me a pamphlet titled "Let's Talk About Sex."

"I want you to be on the pill," she told me. "I'll leave you to read this, okay? I'll come back to talk to you about it later, okay?"

***

I read the pamphlet.

***

When she came back I immediately asked her, "How do girls get pregnant?"

She squinted at me. "I'm sorry?"

"How do girls get pregnant?" I repeated.
She told me.
"Oh," I said.
She frowned. "You didn't know how you got pregnant?"
"No," I replied.
"Oh honey."

***

Nobody came to pick me up when the hospital released me.
I didn't have a change of clothes. I had to put the pajama pants
that I came in back on.

***

It was a three hour walk home.
People pulled over. "What happened to your pants?" they asked
me.
"I was pregnant and the baby died."
"What happened to your pants?" asked a woman driving a
minivan.
"I was pregnant and the baby died."
"What happened to your pants?" asked a man driving a con-
vertible.
"I was pregnant and the baby died."
"What happened to your pants?" asked a kid playing with toy
trucks in his driveway.
"I was pregnant and the baby died."

***

When I got home my mom and dad were smoking in the front
room.
"How do girls get pregnant?" I shouted at them as soon as I
walked within their earshot.

They both looked at me. "What the hell are you wearing that for Samantha?"

I looked at the blood all over my pants.

"Because," I said through my teeth, "you didn't bring me a change of clothes. Or come pick me up."

"Don't you dare talk to us with that fucking attitude—" my mom started.

"Because," I shouted, "you didn't bring me a change of clothes. Or come pick me up."

"Because you didn't bring me a change of clothes or come pick me up."

"Because you didn't bring me a change of clothes or come pick me up."

"Because you didn't bring me a change of clothes or come pick me up."

***

"Want an apple juice?" a nurse asks me.

"No."

"We have popsicles. Would you like a popsicle?"

"No."

"Do you know how to work the T.V.?"

I glare. "Yes. I am familiar with how to work a T.V. Despite all of the odds stacked against me, I have managed to successfully master the technical skills required to operate a television. Thank you."

***

I have been transferred to a special section of the hospital. I am being detained here until someone with authority grants me my freedom. I learned that this process cannot be hastened by punching a nurse.

The patients in this ward are all suffering from some sort of psychological circumstance. My circumstance is apparently clinical depression. Not usually one to contest the analysis of a trained professional, I believe that I have been misdiagnosed. The only thing that I am depressed about is being in here.

***

"Undress!" a nurse shouts at me as she enters the room.

I stare at her.

"Undress!" she repeats loutishly, apparently enjoying herself. "Undress! Undress! Undress!"

Unenthusiastic about stripping for free in front of this disconcerting stranger, I cross my arms.

"Do I have to do it in front of you?" I ask defiantly.

"It's nothing that I haven't seen before," she sings, holding out the hospital clothing that she wants me to change into.

"Whether you have seen a naked person before does not really matter to me," I explain, snatching the clothing from her. "Believe it or not, my aversion towards undressing in front of you has nothing to do with fearing that you have never seen a naked human body before."

I am speaking very clearly and I am projecting my voice. I am not yelling or using a violent tone. Unfortunately, being assertive when you are in a position of subordination, such as the position of "patient", unsettles others. It implies that you do not respect their authority, that you do not respect authority structures in general, and that you are, therefore, an unpredictable loose cannon. Alternatively, it can lead to your being treated like a child.

"Unfortunately, no, I can't leave you alone. Are you going to undress by yourself, or do other measures need to be taken?"

"Other measures?" I repeat her, "does that mean that if I don't undress in front of you, you will have someone forcefully take my clothes off?"

Her silent response implies that this is indeed the protocol.

"Are you going to undress now or not?"

"Yes." I scowl at her. "Should I do it slowly for you?"

She rolls her eyes.

"Is there a table that I could stand on to make this experience more enjoyable for the both of us?"

She rolls her eyes again.

***

Had I not been suicidal prior to my hospital visit, I would be now. My clothing has been confiscated and, in what feels like a personal attack, I am now being forced to wear a paper dress embellished with several illustrations of Snoopy the dog. In fact, they may not even be Snoopy. On closer inspection, they appear to be drawings of a knock-off, off-brand Snoopy.

I am now being led like a cow to an examination room, for God knows what next horror. Hopefully this is the room that they use to murder people.

I enter the examination room with my arms hanging limp from my Snoopy-clad shoulders.

A man brandishing a clipboard greets me. He says, "Hello there, Jane."

"Hello." I nod at him.

"Please take off your clothing."

"What?"

"You'll have to undress. I need to examine your injuries."

I stare at him, purse my lips, and tilt my head backwards.

He stares at me.

"Fine!" I scream after a soundless moment has passed, startling the man so much so that he drops his clipboard.

I begin to undress myself, exuding as much hostility as I can muster. Unfortunately my efforts distract me from the task in hand, and I manage to tangle myself up. I struggle to pull the dress up over my head. I have to pause, stomach and chest exposed, with the dress wrapped around my face to catch my unstoppable, never-ending, persevering breath.

***

After being sworn into the psych ward via a process more intricate and draining than the inauguration of a president, I am now sitting on yet another hospital bed in yet another room.

"When do I get to leave?" I ask a nurse.

"I don't know," she answers, handing me a cup of room-temperature water.

"How long do people normally stay here?"

"I don't know."

"Do you know anything?"

***

I have to share a room. I am expected to sleep mere meters from a woman whose mental ailment is unknown to me. For all I know she might be a cannibal.

She has drawn my attention by frequently cradling all of her belongings in her arms and glaring at me. I think that she suspects that I am a kleptomaniac.

Your half-used stick of deodorant and your Styrofoam cup are not worth stealing, cannibal lady. If you hadn't treated me like an untrustworthy criminal, I would have never considered taking your things. Now, because of your presumptuous behaviour, I can't think of anything but robbing you blind.

***

I watch the sky through my window transform from black to navy to blue. Once the sky has been blue for a few hours, I hear my roommate roll over, stand up, and leave.

I ignore the nurses when they tell me to eat. I stay in my bed until it is nighttime again.

***

I watch the sky through my window transform from black to navy to blue again.

***

"You have to eat while you're in here," a nurse tells me.
I roll over in my bed so that I'm facing the wall away from her.

***

"You're expected to attend therapy sessions," another nurse tells me.
I roll over in my bed so that I'm facing the wall away from her.
I listen to two nurses talk outside my room about how sad it is that I have no next of kin.
"Her parents are both dead," they say too loudly, apparently assuming I am asleep.
"She doesn't have anybody."

***

A new morning comes, despite my concerted lack of desire for it to do so. I lift myself with the bad-mannered sun from the uncomfortable hospital bed. My bones make cracking noises.
I stand up and walk over to my roommate's side table. I take her deodorant and her cup.
I then emerge from the room in search of a washroom. I throw my roommate's belongings into the first garbage bin that I cross paths with.

I reach my destination only to discover that the bathrooms here have no doors.

"Excuse me." I stop the first hospital employee that I see.

I have not spoken in more than two days and my voice is raw.

I clear my throat. "Where is the door to this washroom?"

"There are no doors to the washrooms in this ward," he explains.

I stare expressionless at him in response.

***

I asked a nurse for dental floss and was told that I am not allowed dental floss. Apparently dental floss can be used for several functions besides the maintenance of healthy gums. These apparently include self-harm. When instructed that I was not permitted dental floss because of "risks it raises associated with suicide" I envisioned a noose made entirely of floss. Realizing such a noose would require a dramatic amount of floss to effectively uphold any human person, I brought it to the attention of a nurse.

"I don't believe that even the most practiced engineers could fashion any functioning noose out of a single container of floss," I say.

"People use it to cut themselves," she explained.

"Oh," I replied.

***

I had just about come to terms with the no-floss rule until the hospital, in a flagrant display of disrespect for its patients, chose to serve us corn on the cob for lunch.

"Are you aware that we are not allowed dental floss?" I yelled at the nurse bringing me the corn. I then threw the corn violently from my plate into the nearest wall.

***

I noticed that the standard hospital shoes that patients are forced to wear have shoelaces. Shoelaces that could be manipulated in much the same way as floss might be used to cut oneself. In light of this observation, the floss issue is back on the table.

***

"Does someone in charge of this hospital have a lot of dentists in their family?" I ask the psychiatrist who I am meeting with.

"What?" he looks at me, confused.

"Does an executive at this hospital have any close ties to someone who profits from mass poor oral health?" I rephrase myself.

"What?" he says again.

"Never mind," I mutter, running my tongue along my back molars.

He shuffles through some papers and sighs.

"Well, you've got quite the file," he comments, leaning back in his chair.

I don't reply.

"You've been diagnosed with clinical depression here, and in the past it says that you've been classified as someone with both intermittent explosive disorder, as well as someone with battered person syndrome."

And soon I will be able to add gum disease to my curriculum vitae of health concerns.

"You've also had issues with drug use. Correct?"

"Yes."

"It sounds like you've had a very difficult life so far, Jane," he says in a pseudo-sympathetic tone. "I am so sorry about that."

"It's been fine," I reply loudly.

"I don't think that you've been given enough support," he continues. "You needed more rehabilitation."

"I have a probation therapist," I tell him. "I see her all of the time."

"I don't know that weekly meetings with a therapist are sufficient."

I don't reply.

"Do you have a support system, Jane? I see you have no living family members. Do you have anyone to help you besides your therapist?"

I don't reply.

"I can see that you have made momentous improvements in the past two years which have led to you to where you are now. Are you struggling with any lingering emotions about your past?"

"No."

***

I am now attending group therapy. This form of therapy is apparently supposed to help me address my issues in a supportive social environment. How airing my private psychological problems in the company of a group of disturbed strangers is supposed to benefit me remains a mystery. I asked why I was put in group therapy, rather than individual therapy, and I was assured that the science behind that decision was sound.

I am more astute a patient than they've guessed, however. I am aware that this decision was not grounded in any prescribed psychological technique, but that it was instead a shrewd business choice. Psychiatrists are paid well. If we patients are all treated as a group it costs the hospital less.

So here I sit, ready to kiss my entire list of mental ailments goodbye thanks to this thrifty, economical treatment.

None of these patients are experiencing the same issues. I am supposed to discuss how I feel sad with a man who is hearing voices, a woman who has to spin eighteen times before sitting down, a feeble, elderly woman with bulimia, and a man who mutters to himself at varying volumes about geography.

"How are you feeling today, Jane?" the meeting facilitator asks me.

"I feel great. Thank you."

"The southern-most portion of Sweden…" the man has begun with whispering today.

"Are you experiencing any dark thoughts?"

Every thought I have had since being in this hospital has been at least loosely associated with murdering someone.

"No."

"So you're feeling much better then?"

"I am, yes."

The psychiatrist smiles at me. "How about you, Edwin? How are you feeling today?"

"Helicopter," Edwin replies.

***

There are Tupperware containers overflowing with condoms on every available counter space in this hospital. The patients here are apparently untameable when it comes to the physical act of love.

I lean on the side of the receptionist's kiosk and ask, "Hey, why are there so many condoms in here?"

She looks up from her papers. "Why? Do you have a latex allergy?"

I make an expression similar to one that might be produced by a person who has consumed expired yogurt.

"I am not interested in having sex with anyone in a psych ward," I shout, insulted by her assumption that my inquiry was grounded in anything other than my own gruesome curiosity.

She raises her eyebrows haughtily, as if I am lying to her.

"Unless you are available?" I bark brashly at her.

She rolls her eyes and tells me to go sit in my room.

"I just wanted to know what the deal was with what seems to me an excessive amount of condoms." I begin to raise my voice. "Can't I even ask a simple question in here?"

She tells me to go sit in my room again.

"I am beginning to have suspicions that we are part of some perverted medical experiment!" I say very loudly, so the other patients in the room can hear, "And I would appreciate your assurance that we are not!"

"Go to your room."

"Is this the set of some hidden camera crazy person fetish porn?" I look around, as if I am trying to spot cameras. "Could you, at a minimum, comfort me by promising that it's not?"

The patients in the room start muttering to each other. The paranoid schizophrenic clique appears to be especially perturbed.

***

I was escorted to my bedroom for being disruptive.

***

"And how are you feeling today, Miss Jane?" the group therapy facilitator asks me.

I take a moment to stifle the feelings I have about being called "Miss Jane", before replying, "I am feeling great. Thank you."

"Are you experiencing any dark thoughts?"

"No," I say while I imagine strangling the facilitator with his own tie.

"Great!"

***

A nurse knocks on the doorframe of my room.

"What?" I look up at her, bothered that she has interrupted my hectic evening of staring out of the window into nothingness and willing my body to die.

"You can use the phone now, if you want to," she informs me before walking quickly away.

I amble out of my room after her. Looking down the hallway to see where she went I am left to assume that she must have already taken on her true form as a bat, as she appears to have vanished.

I don't know where the phone is kept.

I wander around the hallway, like a child lost at a mall, aimlessly searching for a hospital employee.

"Hello?"

"Hello?"

"Hello? I was told I can use the phone but I don't know where the phone is kept. Do you know?" I ask a group of patients who are walking by.

They whisper to each other and ignore me.

"Hello, I was told I could use the phone but I don't know where the phone is kept. Do you know where it is?" I ask an elderly man sitting on the ground outside of the bathroom.

He stares at me and says nothing.

A nurse emerges from a doorway.

"Hello!" I wave at her. "Hello, I was told that I could use the phone but I don't know where the phone is kept! Could you please show me—"

"I'm too busy!" she yells, while powerwalking in the opposite direction.

I watch her exit through a glass door at the end of the hallway. I watch as she stands just outside of the door, lights a cigarette, tilts her head backwards, and exhales up into the sky.

***

"And how is my star patient, Jane?" The group therapy facilitator asks me.

The other patients' eyes all turn towards me.

"I'm doing great, thank you." I lie.

"You are doing fantastic!" he shouts like he's performing a high school cheer. "Are you experiencing any dark thoughts?"

"No."

"Great!" He punches the air triumphantly.

***

"The phone is available if you still need to use it!" a nurse croons into my room while prancing by.

"Where is the phone kept?" I shout back at her, but she has already vanished.

Rather than waste my energy struggling to stop her, I instead use it to roll over in my bed.

***

I dream that my stomach is round and swollen. I run my hands along the taut curve and up to my smoke-burnt chest. I cross my arms and rock myself to the familiar noise of crashing dishes, my father yelling, and my mother screaming. All of this lulls me into a deeper and more contented sleep.

Keats' face appears next to my childhood bed. He opens his enormous mouth and whispers, "Maybe you'll get a cool scar."

Ivy's face pops up next to his, frowning.

"Scars are cool, Ivy," he explains to her, "they add character."

My phone keeps ringing.

"Hello?" I pick it up.

"You've got cuts all over you," a voice points out. "Do you do that to yourself?"

I can hear my feet slapping against tile. The soles of my feet are sore.

"Where are you going?" a nurse asks me.

I look at her, desperate to communicate without words that I need to be let out of this hospital.

"Are you okay, honey?"

"Yes," I lie.

***

"The phone is free if you need to use it," a nurse tells me from the hall outside my room.

"Cool," I reply, and stay where I am.

***

"How are you feeling today, Jane?"

"I feel good, thank you."

"Are you experiencing any dark thoughts?"

"No."

***

"We have contacted your therapist," the psychiatrist informs me sternly from over his clipboard. "You are to meet with him immediately, and your appointments with him will become more frequent now."

"My therapist is a woman," I correct him.

"Oh," he pauses, shuffling through his papers. "Right. Yes. Of course. Also, your medication is going to change now."

"Alright."

"We have to stagger your prescriptions too, so you'll only be getting a few pills at time. Do you understand why we're doing that?"

I stare into his face before replying.

"Yes, I understand," I say, successfully repressing a strong impulse to reply sarcastically. What possible reason could he have for not giving me, a patient who recently ate a pound of pills, an excessive supply of more pills?

"Do you have any questions for me?"

"No."

***

I am escorted out of the hospital, a cured woman. Entirely recovered from that which ailed me. All of my demons shredded. Normal and healthy and well.

***

I walk into my apartment. Upon entering, I find Keats sitting at the kitchen table. He is surrounded by piles of my belongings. My clothes, paperwork, cellphone, and miscellaneous possessions are all stacked around him and are all being painstakingly inspected.

"What are you doing?" I ask quietly.

He drops the piece of paper in his hand, stands up quickly, and looks at me.

"You're back," he says breathlessly.

"What are you doing with all of my stuff?" I ask, remaining calm.

"I'm looking for information," he says in an unsteady voice.

"You're not going to find any information."

"Did you really try to kill yourself?" he asks me quickly.

"No," I lie, "of course not."

***

My phone rings.

"Hello."

"Hello, am I speaking with Jane?"

"Yes. Who is this?"

"This is George. I'm a Krippler Incorporated representative. I'm calling because we've noticed that you've missed about a week of work. Is this your way of quitting?"

"Oh," I say. "I'm sorry, no. I've just been sick. I've had no access to a phone until today."

"I see," he replies.

"I had a severe allergic reaction to pine nuts," I explain. "I went into anaphylactic shock, and unfortunately I had to be hospitalized. I was unconscious for more than a day. When I was finally awake the doctors wanted me to stay under observation—for safety, you know? I didn't have my cell phone on me so I couldn't call, and it is very difficult to use the hospital phone nowadays, did you know that?"

"Oh, no I had no idea. Are you feeling better now?"

"I'm doing okay," I clear my throat, "I guess it's difficult to use the phone nowadays because it's expected that everyone has a cell phone. I didn't have mine on me when I had the reaction and so I was out of luck, you know? I apologize for not calling. I should have asked someone to call on my behalf. I was so preoccupied and distracted in the hospital."

"Please, there's no need to apologize. That's okay. You can take more medical leave if you need to. We only want you to come back to us when you feel well enough, alright?"

"Okay, thank you."

"You should do whatever you need to do for your own health. Your health matters to us, alright?"

"Okay, thank you."

"Unfortunately, it, uh, can't be paid leave," he adds slowly.

"Is Frank still fired?" I ask.

"Who?"

"Never mind."

***

Rather than stew unpaid in the failure of my suicide, I have opted to resume my post at Krippler Incorporated. My desk has been moved since my last shift. It is now beside the washrooms. The happy privilege of knowing my co-workers' toilet schedules has been bestowed upon me. My new location is also adjacent to a large motivational poster. It reads: "Every strike brings me closer to the next home run." This is something Babe Ruth, a notorious alcoholic and adulterer, once said. I am entertaining the idea that my suicide attempt was successful and that I am in Hell.

***

"Hello my name is—"
They hang up.
"Hello my name is—"
They hang up.
"Hello my name is—"
They hang up.
"Hello my name is—"
They hang up.

***

"Hello, my name is Jane. I am calling on behalf of—"
"Are you kidding me?"
"Krippler Incorporated. Today we are conducting a survey—"
"I had hoped that you'd finally given up on harassing me," the respondent groans. "I thought that this hellish interaction between us was finally over. I had hoped that maybe you'd died."
        "Today we are conducting—"
"Today is going to be the last time that you EVER call my house, you small-minded, and painfully oblivious girl-child. Do you understand me? Can you please try to direct the blood from your hell-mouth uterus up to your simple brain for a moment long enough to register what I am saying?"
"We are conducting a survey on feline diabetes."
"If you call me ever again I will retaliate," he spits, "do not think that I won't."
"Do you or any member of your household own a cat?"
"Call me one more goddamn time," he snarls. "Just try it!"
After he hangs up I dial his number again.
"Hello, this is a girl-child calling on behalf of…"

***

My phone keeps ringing.

"Hello?"

"Jane?"

"Yes?"

They hang up.

"Hello?"

"Jane?"

"Yes?"

They hang up.

***

I wake up at 3:00 a.m. to the trying sound of my phone vibrating again.

"Hello?" I breathe into it.

"Are you home?" the voice in my phone asks me.

"Why? Who is this?"

They hang up.

I roll over and close my eyes. The dulcet resonance of Keats' murmurings into his own cell phone keeps me alert. Despite every effort I make to tune him out, I still manage to overhear him use my name, and say something about sending hair scrounged from my comb to a lab.

"I know a guy who works in a university lab," he fails to whisper. "He told me he could examine her hair and tell me who she really is."

I like to think that I have a high level of patience for Keats' idiosyncrasies; however, when he introduces chemists into the equation, I find it difficult to remain collected.

"I dare you to touch my hair brush," I shout firmly from my bed.

He starts murmuring faster into his phone.

Concerned that the mental illness afflicting Keats could be airborne, I resolve to leave the apartment.

***

I walk through the front door and light a cigarette.

As I inhale, a voice addresses me.

"Jane?" it says.

I stare into the darkness for a face.

"Hello?"

"Jane?"

"Yes?"

"I am so sorry to bother you," a man steps into the street light. "I would just absolutely hate to bother you."

He is leering at me. I examine his face to assess if I have ever seen him before.

I haven't.

"I'm not bothering you, am I?" he asks me, leaning in slightly.

"Who are you?" I squint at him.

He widens his eyes, exposing the white around his irises. "I am someone who you have asked a sufficient amount questions."

I maintain eye contact with him.

He walks a little closer to me.

"Does my voice sound familiar?" he asks, leaning closer still. "Does it perhaps ring a bell?"

I shrug and inhale from my cigarette.

"I am the man that you have been calling every day for months." He grins at me. "I am the victim of your GODDAMN PERPET-UAL FUCKING PHONE CALLS!" He screams hysterically.

He then smiles and says quietly, "That's who I am."

He takes his hand out of his pocket and extends it towards me. "I am so pleased to finally meet you in person."

I look at his hand and then back at his face.

He smiles wider and takes another step towards me.

"Remember me now, do you Jane?"

I nod. "Sure."

"You should have listened to me," he whispers. "You should have stopped goddamn calling me when I goddamn asked you to."

I press my lips together. "Please accept my apology."

He laughs hard.

He laughs so hard he has to hold his sides.

His face becomes enflamed and damp.

"Hahahaha."

"Hahahahahahah."

"Ha ha ha ha ha ha ha!"

He starts to do a fake laugh. "Ha," he says seriously, "ha—ha—ha." He locks his eyes with mine.

"How did you like being called by me incessantly?" he asks, puffing out his chest.

"Was that you?"

"HOW DID YOU LIKE BEING RELENTLESSLY BOTH-ERED!" he shrieks, ignoring my question.

He pulls his other hand out of his pocket and I notice the handle of a gun peering over the lip of his belt.

I step backwards.

"Listen, I'm sorry—" I begin to say.

"I don't care if you're sorry," he snarls and starts grabbing at me. I try to get away but he snatches at me, his hands snapping at me like the jaws of a shark.

He grips the top of my arm and jerks me violently towards him.

"Don't touch me," I shout, as loud as I can.

He grips my other arm.

I twist his wrist with one arm and push the end of my cigarette into the side of his face with the other. I am screaming. He tries to pin me to the ground but struggles while I bite the skin on the side of his face. I bite his ear so hard that it tears partially off when he jerks his head back away from me. He is screaming and grabbing fistfuls of my hair and my scalp in his hands. I shove his head sideways and twist his body until I am able to restrain him. I get hold of the gun. I can't feel anything. I close my eyes and punch him in the face until my muscles tire and I am gasping for air.

"Stop!" he's crying.

"Please stop!"

I open my eyes. There's blood all over my pants.

***

There's blood all over my pants.

***

"Because," I say through my teeth, "you didn't bring me a change of clothes. Or come pick me up."

I disengage the safety on the gun.

"Because you didn't bring me a change of clothes or come pick me up."

"Because you didn't bring me a change of clothes or come pick me up."

"Because you didn't bring me a change of clothes or come pick me up."

About The Author

Emily was born in 1989 and grew up in St. Thomas, Ontario, Canada. She studied English Language and Literature at the University of Western Ontario and she got an MA in Library and Information Science. She currently lives in Ottawa.

Acknowledgements

Thank you Corrina and Gloria for your writerly influence. Mallory and Ainsley, you have both been like sisters to me. Thank you Aaron for upping the odds that I get diabetes, and for being precious. Thank you to my uncle Joe who collects pens. You are my favourite uncle, but don't tell your brothers. Christina and Matthew, thank you for turning this quiet, cross-eyed girl with no friends into a quiet, cross-eyed girl with two friends. And thank you Brock, for opting for eye uncrossing surgery. Thank you Bridget, who should write a book herself. Thanks also to "Jacob Marley", my English and writing teachers at the University of Western Ontario, as well as the English teachers at St. Joseph's High School. Thank you to both Robert Peett and Natasha Robson at Holland House for publishing this book, and for seeing me through the whole process. I am grateful to you both. If I forgot to name you, thank you especially for your forgiveness.

9 781910 688250